I0817959

GIRL FOUR:
LURED

(A Maya Gray FBI Suspense Thriller—Book 4)

Molly Black

Molly Black

Debut author Molly Black is author of the MAYA GRAY FBI suspense thriller series, comprising six books (and counting); and the RYLIE WOLF FBI suspense thriller series, comprising three books (and counting).

An avid reader and lifelong fan of the mystery and thriller genres, Molly loves to hear from you, so please feel free to visit www.mollyblackauthor.com to learn more and stay in touch.

ISBN: 978-1-0943-9361-2

BOOKS BY MOLLY BLACK

MAYA GRAY MYSTERY SERIES

GIRL ONE: MURDER (Book #1)
GIRL TWO: TAKEN (Book #2)
GIRL THREE: TRAPPED (Book #3)
GIRL FOUR: LURED (Book #4)
GIRL FIVE: BOUND (Book #5)
GIRL SIX: FORSAKEN (Book #6)

RYLIE WOLF FBI SUSPENSE THRILLER

FOUND YOU (Book #1)
CAUGHT YOU (Book #2)
SEE YOU (Book #3)

CHAPTER ONE

Maya stood in the middle of the barn, feeling a brief note of relief as she stared down at the woman on the stretcher. The rest of an FBI team stood around her, clearing the area, making sure that there were no traps or bombs.

She'd been sent to recover the Moonlight Killer's most recent hostage, leaning in close to the stretcher, desperate to hear the message that the young woman there had brought from her sister. Katya's words came out as little more than a whisper.

"He has a tattoo on his forearm: a snake crushing an armadillo under a full moon."

Those words sent a shock through Maya as she realized that for the first time, she had something beyond the most basic physical information on the Moonlight Killer, the man who had taken her sister and eleven other women hostage.

Eight in total now. He was only holding eight women. Maya had secured the release of three of them by solving the murders he'd sent her off to investigate, while one had found herself killed for trying to escape.

That last thought filled her with fear for her sister. Megan had taken a huge risk, trying to get this information to Maya. If the Moonlight Killer realized what she'd done, then even that might be enough to get her killed.

That was why Maya knew that she couldn't share it with her superiors, not yet. The same way that she hadn't shared with them the real identity of the man who'd kidnapped so many women. She couldn't take any chance of the information slipping out, and the Moonlight Killer heard far too much.

Talking of her boss, Deputy Director Harris was currently standing just a few paces away, looking over at Maya with obvious expectation. The deputy director was an avuncular middle-aged man with slightly soft features, a shaved head designed to hide his bald spot, and an expensive suit under his tactical jacket.

"Well?"

He wanted to know what the message had been, but Maya knew that she couldn't just come out and say it. The deputy director had jumped on clues before, pushing forward in ways that had gotten people hurt, that had gotten her *sister* hurt.

More than that though, Maya was increasingly convinced that the Moonlight Killer was listening in to every word that she said. She had to be careful now what she said aloud, and to whom.

"She just confirmed that my sister is alive and well, trapped together with the others," Maya said. It was a lie, but it was the kind of lie that was plausible enough that Harris might not double check.

"We knew that," Harris looked a little deflated.

It felt wrong, lying to her boss like that. It *was* wrong. If it came out, it could cost Maya her job or worse. It could see her face charges for obstruction of justice. Yet honestly, Maya didn't know what else to do. The alternative was far, far worse.

"Still, we have something," Harris said, looking brighter. "If Katya here really believes that she knows where she was brought here from, we might actually have a chance to *catch* the man who's doing all this. We need to get back and start working on this at once."

*

Back on the fourth floor of the FBI headquarters, Maya was getting a horrible feeling of déjà vu. Out in the bullpen of the fourth floor, surrounded by desks, Harris was standing in the midst of a large group of agents, with a board set out in the middle, a map on that board.

A plan was starting to form there, and Maya knew another raid building up when she saw one.

"We managed to get some information from the hostage," Harris said. "We've also had forensics back on one of the early postcards that the kidnapper sent. No personal traces, but there were microscopic plant spores that can help us narrow an area down."

Around him, the other agents looked on as if they hadn't listened to all this before, as if they'd simply forgotten the two previous raids Harris had organized, and the consequences. As if they hadn't been there for the planning of the attempt to catch the Moonlight Killer when he released his first hostage, or for the raid on an empty building that had seen SWAT team members walk into claymore mines, or for the second raid, which had seen her sister systematically beaten by the

Moonlight killer after it had failed, and photographs sent to Maya as proof.

Or maybe they didn't care. Agent Reyes stood near Harris, younger than Maya, Latino, of middling height. He looked as eager as ever to play his part in catching the kidnapper, but then, he'd been one of the ones pushing for it from the start of all this.

Maya didn't know if that was just the desire to get all this done, or if he wanted the glory of catching this guy all to himself. Either way, it was dangerous.

"We believe we have a location," Harris said, pointing to a specific spot. He moved over to aerial photographs set out on the board to the side of the map. They showed a building, some kind of wooden cabin, obviously custom built. "This is the location we will be focusing on with our raid. If we strike quickly, I believe that we can capture this guy before he can react."

Maya couldn't hold her anger back any longer. She walked out into the middle of them, as tall as Harris, dark haired, wearing a suit today, but it didn't do much to disguise the athleticism of her build. She could only guess at how much of the anger she felt was showing on her face but judging from the way Harris's eyes narrowed as she approached, Maya guessed that at least some of it did.

"Sir, may I speak to you privately?"

Harris shook his head. "I already have a good idea of what you're going to say, Grey."

Maybe that should have been Maya's cue to keep quiet, but she couldn't, not today.

"That we've been here before?" Maya said. "That we've gone in headfirst after leads on the kidnapper twice now, and both times, it turns out that he was setting us up to remind us that we shouldn't break the rules of his little game?"

She had to remind herself to just call him the kidnapper, and not the Moonlight Killer. It was another facet of this that she'd chosen to hold back, and now really wasn't the time to reveal it. If Harris knew who they were actually chasing, nothing would stop him from putting all his efforts into the hunt, rather than saving the women the Moonlight Killer still held.

"Those times were different," Harris said. He actually sounded as if he meant it. The deputy director was an intelligent man, so how could he keep falling into the same trap?

Maya cocked her head to one side. "How?"

"Because those times, it was with information he could control. The latest hostage, Katya, has a good sense of time and direction. She knows where she was. Tell me how he fakes that, Grey."

Maya paused, trying to work it out. She had to admit that Harris had a point: it was the kind of thing that seemed hard to fake, yet she was also sure that with enough time and preparation, it might be possible.

That was the thing about this whole situation: they were always playing catchup, having to move quickly. Whereas the Moonlight Killer had demonstrated exactly how cunning he could be.

"We have the full resources of the FBI," Reyes said. "He's just one guy."

"Just one guy who's had months to plan this," Maya pointed out. That was the difference. "Our resources don't count for anything if we have only hours to try to counter something that he's been planning and putting into motion for who only knows how long."

"So you want to just sit back and do nothing?" Reyes countered. "You want to keep just solving crimes for him? Giving him what he wants?"

That seemed a little harsh, coming from him.

Maya rounded on him. "And how many women have your efforts saved, Reyes? My way has gotten us back three women."

"And gotten one killed."

It was stupid and embarrassing, arguing in front of so many other agents, but it seemed that this was what Maya's career had come to by this point. She also didn't have another choice, when Harris wouldn't take this to his office.

"The woman who was killed died because she tried to escape. Whereas I have *detailed* photographs of what the kidnapper did to my sister as a warning the last time we tried this."

Harris switched to a calmer voice. "It's because your sister is caught up in this that you can't be objective about it, Grey. We have a kidnapper who has hurt and killed his captives. Even if that wasn't down to what we're doing, it suggests that the situation is unstable. We have to act to stop him."

Maya couldn't deny that part. The moment she'd found Carmel's body, she'd thought that the whole situation was spiraling out of control. The Moonlight Killer had sent one of his seemingly endless postcards to explain it, but Maya couldn't deny how dangerous the whole situation was.

"This still seems like a bad idea," Maya said, gesturing to the board. "We've tried this twice now. Doing the same thing again seems like a good way to just get more women hurt. For the moment, our best option seems to be to keep solving the murders as he sends them."

Harris was already shaking his head. "That's not an acceptable option, Grey. I will not sit here and play the game of someone who has already shown that he is willing to kill. Unless you can come up with a better option, I suggest you go back to your desk and allow us to get on with planning this raid."

Maya wanted to argue, but she could see from the set expression on Harris's face that it wasn't going to achieve anything. There was a stoniness to it that Maya knew all too well. She'd come so close to being thrown off the team in the last few days that she suspected that, if she pushed this too far, she might find herself transferred to another department, or simply suspended. If she wasn't there, then she couldn't do anything to help.

For now, all she could do was retreat from the planning, trying to think of something that might make a difference here. Was there anything that Maya could do to change Harris's mind? Anything more that might make any kind of difference? Could she just slap the photographs of Megan's injuries down in front of Harris to remind him of the stakes? Could she bring up Carmel's death again, or one of the postcards that had brought a warning with it?

No, that wouldn't change anything. Would telling him about the tattoo? It might show Harris that there might be a way to find the kidnapper beyond charging after him based on what Katya remembered. No, that wouldn't dissuade Harris from the raid; it would just make him ask why she hadn't mentioned it before.

What else was there? There was a brief, stupid temptation to get out her phone and state the details of the raid into it, knowing that the Moonlight Killer was almost certainly listening in. If she warned the Moonlight Killer about what was coming, maybe it would buy safety for her sister and the other hostages.

Maya couldn't bring herself to do that, though. It wasn't just that it was a crime to give away the details of a FBI investigation like that, it was that Maya couldn't stand the thought of helping a killer. Besides, what if he used the information to set a trap, rather than to escape? What if he used the information to kill? Maya couldn't do it.

Which meant that she needed another plan. What plan, though? What could she possibly do that would make any of this better? The only possible answer to that came to Maya, and she didn't like it, but she knew that there was no real alternative.

She could sit at her desk doing nothing, or she could be at the heart of this, controlling the situation as best she could. Maya stood and carefully set her phone down on her desk before she made her way back towards the deputy director. Harris saw her coming, and was already shaking his head as Maya approached.

"If you want in on this mission, you're out of luck, Grey. I need people who aren't too invested in this to be able to think clearly."

"You said to come to you if I had a better option," Maya said, taking her opportunity. "I do."

"You think that after a couple of minutes' thought you have a better idea than we've been able to come up with?" Reyes said. Maya could hear the disbelief there, and the hostility.

"Yes," Maya said, simply. "Because my plan is one that we haven't already tried, where we know it doesn't work."

"And what is your plan?" Harris said.

"Solo reconnaissance." This was the part that was going to be hard to sell them on. They were used to working as a large team, deploying all the resources at their disposal to solve problems.

Harris looked interested, though. "Elaborate."

"A single agent approaches the site on foot. They're more likely to remain undetected, and can try to establish if this is actually an empty building or not. If we establish for sure that he really is there, then they can call in backup and take him. If it's another empty building, they can back off, and the kidnapper is none the wiser that we were ever there. There's no risk to the hostages, and we don't lose out on any potential chance to catch the guy who's doing this."

Maya could see Harris mulling it over, tapping his fingers together as he thought.

"It does have advantages over a full raid," he agreed. "But there are dangers. A single agent might not be enough to take the kidnapper down if they run into trouble. It's not something that I would feel comfortable asking any of the agents here to do."

Maya had guessed that Harris might say something like that. He might be willing to risk the hostages for the sake of getting them back, but he wasn't going to throw his agents away needlessly.

Maya took a breath. "That's why I want to volunteer to be the one who does this."

CHAPTER TWO

Maya crouched silently in her tactical gear, almost invisible against the background of the forest. She timed her breaths to keep her heartbeat low as she watched the cabin from the trees, not wanting to move closer until she was sure that it was the right place.

"Agent Grey, report," Harris said in her earpiece.

It was one compromise she'd had to agree to. Harris might be willing to sanction her going in alone, but he wasn't going to let her be completely out of contact.

"I'm at the location," Maya replied. "It's too early to determine if there's anyone inside."

Patience mattered at a moment like this. Waiting and watching counted. Maya had spent plenty of time scouting locations in her time in the army, and on stakeouts as an agent. Rushing led to mistakes. Sometimes the only thing to do was stay still and observe.

The cabin ahead was large and looked custom built to Maya, clearly a step or two beyond anything just thrown together by the inhabitants. It had two floors, along with a balcony, large windows facing onto the rest of the clearing it sat in, and a couple of small outbuildings that might have been used for storage. Maya saw cameras watching the approaches to the house. Who would need that many of them out here? A flicker of suspicion flared in her at that. Could they have the right place after all?

"We have satellite thermal imagery," Harris said in her ear. Maya didn't want to think about what it must have taken to get that. "It suggests that there is at least one heat signature in the building."

"One?" That wasn't enough. "There should be multiple signatures from the hostages."

"If he's keeping them underground, that might block it," Harris pointed out.

Meaning that Maya still couldn't discount the possibility of this being real. She kept still, resisting the urge to brush a strand of dark hair out of her eyes, ignoring the tension running through her tall, athletic frame as she crouched there. She knew how easy any movement was to pick up on, and didn't want to risk it unnecessarily.

"Can you get into position to see through the windows?" Harris asked.

"Will do," Maya replied, because if she was going to confirm the presence of the Moonlight Killer, then this was really the only way.

It seemed that she didn't have a choice about moving, so she started to creep around, keeping low and trying to use the underbrush to hide her movements.

She tried to move in small flurries, the way an animal might have, pausing between each one to check whether there had been a reaction from the house. Little by little, Maya moved into position in front of the large French windows on one side of the house.

There was someone there.

A man moved around the place, cooking in an open plan kitchen, with his back to Maya. He was tall and dark haired, muscled and probably in his thirties. He wore all black, with a camouflage jacket slung over the back of one of the chairs in the kitchen. When he turned Maya's way, his features were handsome but unremarkable. Maya tried looking for a tattoo, but the long sleeves of his dark shirt made it impossible to tell.

Was *this* the Moonlight Killer? Was this the man who had her sister, and who had killed so many women? Maya knew it was impossible to tell just by looking at him. That was the point: a serial killer like the Moonlight Killer could walk in anywhere, could walk right past someone he was planning to kill, and no one would know who he was.

"Do you have eyes on the target?" Harris asked through her earpiece.

Maya could feel her blood pumping faster. "There's someone here. A man. He appears to be alone. No sign of suspicious activity, though."

"That doesn't matter," Harris said. "This is the location we got from the last hostage."

Maya couldn't deny that, when Katya, the young woman whose release Maya had secured by solving the last crime the Moonlight Killer had sent her to look at, had turned out to have an almost perfect sense of where she'd been. She knew which direction she'd been taken in, and for how long.

This was the place. Did that mean that the other hostages were all here? That her sister was there somewhere? That the man in front of her might actually be the Moonlight Killer? Maya had assumed that this would all be another one of his tricks, but this definitely didn't *look* like another empty house, filled with traps.

"We're going to move in," Harris said, and Maya could hear the determination there. "Backup is on the way. ETA five minutes. Do not lose sight of the target."

Maya had no intention of doing so. As the man she now suspected might be the Moonlight Killer moved around his cabin home, Maya kept pace with him, watching, feeling the tension inside her build as she waited for the opportunity to take him down once and for all.

A radio click in her earpiece alerted her to the arrival of the tactical team sent to help with the arrest. They were in full combat gear, obviously ready for whatever resistance they might meet. Their leader looked across to Maya, the message clear: this was her operation, and she got to make the calls.

She nodded, and gestured them all forward.

With the cameras there, there was no way to cover the ground unseen, so once they broke from the tree line, the only thing to do was move forward quickly with weapons raised, trying to close the gap before the man in the house could react.

He turned and spotted them when they were three quarters of the way to the cabin, and Maya saw the sudden fear of his reaction. He turned, heading deeper into the house.

Terror sprang up in Maya then as she realized where he might be going. Was he trying to get to the hostages? Trying to kill them just to deprive Maya of the chance of getting her sister back? Maya wouldn't let that happen. She *couldn't.*

Lifting her Glock, she fired twice at the French windows. They shattered into fragments, the safety glass splintering into a thousand pieces and falling away even as Maya burst through into the cabin. Inside, it was sparsely furnished except for some hunting trophies, with a few pieces of antique looking furniture scattered here and there and hand knotted rugs on the floor.

Maya was moving too quickly to take it all in. She ran after the fleeing figure of the man, following him through into a dining area where an assault weapon hung up above a fireplace. The man was reaching for it, and Maya threw herself forward, slamming the butt of her Glock into the back of his head to send him sprawling to the ground.

She stood over him with the weapon levelled, and in that moment, Maya wanted nothing more than to empty the rest of her clip into the man who had caused so much misery for so many. The urge was almost overwhelming, and Maya found herself willing him to reach for some unseen weapon, just to give her an excuse.

"Don't move!" Maya ordered him.

The only move the man made, though, was to rub his head where Maya had hit him. "Ow! That wasn't meant to be a part of this! No one said anything about me being hit!"

Maya stood there, trying to make sense of those words. "What do you mean? Where are the hostages?"

"D-downstairs, in the basement."

Maya could hear the fear in his voice, and she found herself caught between satisfaction and confusion in that moment. Satisfaction, because she *wanted* the man who'd kidnapped her sister to be afraid; confusion, because she hadn't expected that the Moonlight Killer would cower from her like this. In her nightmares, he'd been a deadly figure stalking her, not some guy who stumbled over his words just because she was pointing a gun at him.

"Show me," Maya ordered. "And if you put a single foot out of place, you're a dead man."

He stood, and Maya kept her Glock trained on him while he started to lead the way through the house.

"Clear and secure the scene," Maya ordered the rest of the tactical team.

They spread out, moving through the rooms. Maya followed her prisoner, watching for any sign that this was all an act, and that he was about to turn the tables on her. So far, though, it seemed that he was just going along meekly with what she'd instructed him to do.

He led the way to a set of steps that led down into a basement area.

"You first," Maya ordered. "And don't try anything."

"Ok, ok," the man said, looking more flustered by the moment.

He led the way down the steps, flicking on a light that burned a low red, casting strange shadows over everything. By that light, Maya saw the cages, looking sinister in the half-dark. She saw the figures standing within them, eight of them now, still in their confinement.

She'd done it. She'd actually found them. Her sister was in there somewhere.

"Megan!" Maya called out.

There was no answer. There wasn't even movement in response.

Everything was too still, and utterly silent. It took Maya a moment or two to realize what she was looking at, and when she did, a deep sense of horror filled her.

Mannequins stood in the cages, rather than women, staring out at the surrounding basement with blank eyes.

"Ok," the man said, turning to her. "I've led you here. I've given up. Does that mean the show is over?"

"Show?" Maya replied. "What show?"

"The show. The reality show."

"*What* reality show?"

Maya could see the look of surprise on her suspect's face as she said that. It mirrored some of the surprise she felt right then.

"*The Hostage*," the man said. "That's what all this is, right?"

"You'd better explain," Maya said.

"I was contacted by the production company. I play the part of the hostage taker, holding onto these mannequins, since we can't exactly get actors in to just sit in cages for the whole run. Then teams have to play games to earn them back, all while trying to find this location."

It sounded like some kind of absurd lie, yet Maya had seen how he'd cowered after she'd hit him. This wasn't a serial killer, ready to use violence at any moment.

"*That's* what you think is going on?" Maya asked.

"And there was this one moment where they wanted to see how people handled a hostage handoff. They got an actor in for that, playing the part of the victim. I had to take her to this barn from here."

Which explained why Katya knew this location. It also explained how the Moonlight Killer had been able to take her to the barn and be in Oregon to kill Wendel Andover.

He'd played her and the FBI again. In spite of their precautions, he'd found a way to play them all. Still, there was one thing she needed to check.

"Show me your forearms," Maya said.

"My what?"

"Your forearms, now."

"Look, don't you think all of this has gone-"

"This is not a game," Maya snapped. "I am actually an FBI agent, and you're working for someone who has actually kidnapped multiple women. When we get out of here, you're going to have to answer a lot of questions if you don't want to be charged as an accessory. Now, show me your forearms."

The actor in front of her blanched, then did as Maya said. There was no sign of a tattoo on his arms. That eliminated the possibility that this was actually the Moonlight Killer, playing a particularly strange game to try to evade capture. No, this was all just a trick.

Or a trap.

That thought came to Maya with memories of the deathtraps the Moonlight Killer had lured them into before. Maya had almost died in at least one of those, because when it came to retribution for breaking his rules, the Moonlight Killer didn't hold back. Even as she thought it, she saw the squat devices sitting in the cells, lights blinking on them. Timers came into life on their fronts, counting down from a minute.

"We need to get out of the building," Maya told the actor. "Run."

"But those are just props," he insisted. "They're not-"

Maya grabbed him and pulled him towards the stairs. "*Run*!"

She hit her earpiece as she sprinted up the stairs, trying to get to safety. "Everyone clear the building, now! It's rigged to explode."

Maya heard the clatter of the team above running for safety, but by that point, all her concentration was on dragging the actor out of there, up the stairs and through the kitchen.

Together they headed for the ruined French windows, running out through them onto the open ground beyond, heading for the trees as fast as they could. They made it halfway before Maya felt the ripple of the expanding explosion, heard the boom of every remaining window in the building blowing out at once. She flung the actor flat, with her over him, hoping that her tactical vest would shield them both from the worst of any shrapnel.

Maya dared a look back. The whole house was ablaze now, and she knew in that moment that they wouldn't be able to get any useful evidence from it. The Moonlight Killer had erased his tracks even as he'd tried to trap them.

"Grey, talk to me," Harris said. "What's going on?"

"It was a trap," Maya said, unable to keep the anger out of her voice. She'd said this couldn't be real. She'd told him that they shouldn't come here. Now she and the members of the tactical team had nearly been killed. All because Harris hadn't listened to her.

Worse, the Moonlight Killer clearly knew that they'd come here. He'd been the one to trigger the bombs. He had to be watching over a video link. He knew what they'd done, knew they'd broken his rules again.

So now, was a woman going to pay the price? Was Megan?

CHAPTER THREE

The man they called Frank wasn't angry; he was disappointed.

He was disappointed that dear Maya, of all people, still didn't respect the rules of the game. Disappointed that she thought that there was any chance he might be caught so easily. Disappointed that she still didn't treat him as seriously as she should.

He sat on a black chair in the circular heart of his bunker, in front of the banks of screens, watching her run from the house with the actor he'd hired. That part had been easier than he'd thought it would be. With the way the media was these days, apparently an out of work actor was only too ready to believe that a show about kidnapping might be a real thing.

Frank sat there, looking over at the spot where an iron ring hung from the arched roof of the room over a clear space with a drain at its center. Was he going to have to kill someone to make a point over this?

Frank had made sure that the threads wouldn't lead back to him. He'd been careful to use third parties to do all the work of pretending to be a production company, had manipulated people to do what he needed them to do. Over the years, Frank had built up quite a collection of people he could get to do what he wanted, using money, or lies, or simply threats.

Maya was just the latest of a long line, in that regard. Still, this particular disappointment hurt more than most. Frank needed to find a way of making his point clear. A death? It was probably warranted, but he already had the problem of finding *one* replacement bunny, without making it two. In any case, he suspected that might provoke her superiors into full revolt against his efforts. No, he needed something else.

Standing, Frank set his mask into place, pulled on his gloves, checked his stun gun, and started to take out the other items he would need. There was gauze, alcohol, a pen, a fresh postcard, and, of course, a knife.

With everything ready, he opened the door to the rest of the bunker and went out to meet his bunnies.

They were out of their hutches, since it was daytime. Frank allowed them that much freedom, mostly because the illusion of kindness made it easier to control them. They were in the large open room that served as the heart of the bunker, huddled up in ones and twos, obviously more frightened than ever after the loss of one of their number. Some of them stared at him as if expecting that he might kill them at any moment.

They clearly didn't understand him at all. They thought he was some kind of madman, but he didn't kill without a reason. Didn't kill on some *whim*. Carmel had earned her death, and what was going to happen now… well, that was Maya's fault, not his.

If people didn't follow the rules, they got what they deserved.

He went to the chair at the heart of it all, setting down the items he'd brought carefully, letting them watch. He took great care to observe their reactions as he set down the knife, noting who recoiled in fear, and who looked at it hungrily, as if it might offer a way out.

"There has been a breach of the rules in the game dear Maya is playing," Frank said. "I had thought that thc FBI would learn its lesson, but no, it seems they are determined to be stubborn."

Frank could see the fear on all their faces now. A couple of them were trembling like the bunnies he'd named them for, looking around as if there might be somewhere to flee. Didn't they know by now that there wasn't? That they couldn't do anything here unless he wanted it to happen?

"And now, I shall need a volunteer," Frank said. He stared at them levelly, one by one, from behind the mask. "Don't be shy, bunnies. A volunteer."

They stood there, trembling, and that was enough to make Frank raise his voice.

"A volunteer, or I will pick *two* of you."

Of course, Megan Grey started to come forward, injured as she was after Frank's last example.

"Not you. No, you see, our volunteer this time gets to be the prize in the next little game, assuming she does what I tell her. And you… well, I want to hang onto you a little longer." He looked around again. "So, who else?"

Finally, one of them stepped forward. Asha van Nies, twenty-three years old, lithe, red haired, with big green eyes that had lost a lot of their old trusting look since she'd come here. Not the one he would have guessed, but clearly eager to get out of there. Eager enough that she would do anything.

"Very well," Frank said. "You want to get out of here, Asha?"

"Yes," she said, after a couple of seconds' hesitation, as if wondering if it might be the wrong answer.

"Well, it can be you who goes next, assuming Maya succeeds. But first, you're the one who has to pay the price for her misdeeds."

Frank could see her steeling herself for it. "Just do it. Whatever it is, just get it over with."

Frank smiled at that, beneath his mask. "Oh, *I'm* not doing anything. You are. The price of being the next one chosen is simple: one finger."

Frank saw her blanch at that, and start to back away, but Frank moved close.

"Too late to back out now, little bunny. You volunteered."

"I… I didn't know."

"I don't care," Frank said. "It doesn't matter what you know, only what you do. It doesn't matter what Agent Grey's reasons were for breaking my rules, only that she did. So you're going to take the knife, and give me one finger, or I will take it, and I will carve you until no one will ever recognize you again."

Frank could see the terror there in her eyes as he said it, the certainty that he would do what he had threatened. That was good, because it made it more likely that she would actually do what he wanted. Fear was just another lever to make sure that people did what Frank needed them to do.

He saw Asha move to the knife slowly, gingerly. He could see the flickers of emotions running across her face. It made him grateful that he was not prey to that kind of indecision and fear in the same way. He saw her face briefly set in determination, and guessed what she was thinking.

"If you think you can kill me with that knife, you're welcome to try, Asha." He took out his stun gun, holding it loosely in his hand. "Of course, when you fail, I'll take *days* killing you. And someone else will still need to do this."

He kept his voice level. He found that the best threats came when he didn't shout, didn't show obvious anger, just made it sound like a fact. Of course, it was. If she attacked him, there was only one way that it would end. Frank watched the words sink in, slowly leeching the fight out of the young woman.

She took the knife and set her left hand on the arm of the chair. He could see her quivering as she held the knife above her little finger.

"It's very sharp," Frank assured her, in a gentle voice.

Still, she hesitated. Frank had anticipated this. He went over to one of the other bunnies there and lashed out with his stun gun, making her cry out in agony.

"Do it," he ordered. When she still hesitated, he used the stun gun on the next of them. "Do it now. If I have to hurt another one…"

He watched Asha bring the knife down sharply, and heard her cry out. The knife went clattering to the floor of the bunker. Frank was there to scoop it up in an instant, making sure that none of his other bunnies ended up with a weapon.

They were staring on with horror, some of them crying, yet she was stony faced, as if she'd needed to retreat into some harsh place within herself in order to do this.

As soon as he'd done that, he went to the injured young woman, taking the amputated finger and putting it in a plastic bag. Almost tenderly, he applied antiseptic and gauze to the wound.

"There," he said softly, almost proudly. "I knew you could do it. When people do what I want, it can be hard, but it's so much better than the alternative. I need Maya to learn that lesson. I'm sure you'll tell her, when you get out of here. *If* you get out of here."

"But you said-"

"I said you would be the next one chosen," Frank pointed out. "Dear Maya still has to solve her case."

He went to sit on his chair, taking up the postcard, and started to write on it. He chose his words carefully, wanting to make his message clear. He didn't want any misunderstandings this time.

Dear Maya, you did this. You have disappointed me. Do not disappoint me again. Still, this is a teachable moment. One I'm sure Christine Weller would appreciate. Maybe you'll learn enough to save the rest of this bunny. You have one week.

It seemed like enough. Slowly, he flipped the card, starting a delicate pen and ink sketch while Asha clutched at her hand, moaning.

"Be quiet," he snapped. "I am trying to concentrate."

When he'd first come up with this plan, Frank had thought that having his bunnies around would be a delight. Honestly, though, the difficulty of keeping them all almost made the whole enterprise more trouble than it was worth.

Almost, but not quite. After all, the vindication that he got out of it was considerable. The waters became less muddy with each case that dear Maya solved, clarifying his purpose, so that perhaps, just perhaps, the world might be able to comprehend the enormity of it.

In truth, Frank doubted that, but maybe Maya would see it, before the end. She'd done well so far, had proved every bit as resourceful as he might have hoped. In so many ways, she was the perfect audience for what he was trying to do.

Frank took his postcard and the finger that was the price of broken rules, taking them back through to his control center. He would get them to Maya soon enough. There were those who could get them where he needed them without being seen. For now, though, he had another matter to attend to:

He didn't have enough bunnies.

He'd planned all of this, every step, and the plan required twelve bunnies. Twelve women, twelve cases, to deal with the most egregious pretenders to his work. Twelve, and no fewer. Any other number… wouldn't be right. Things *had* to be right.

Carmel had complicated things the moment she'd seen his face. In that moment, she'd made it so that Frank had to kill her. Anything that could identify him with any certainty was too much. Any*one* who could identify him had to die, because that was one of the rules that kept him safe. Yet in dying, Carmel had complicated his plans almost as much as she might have by escaping. It left a hole in them that had to be plugged, an absence that required a replacement.

Of course, Frank had considered this contingency. From the very start of this, when he'd had his bunker built and started to set wheels in motion, he'd been aware that he might lose one of his bunnies. One might die unexpectedly. One might drive him to kill her. One might even escape, although that was far less likely than the other options. From the very start of this, he'd been aware that he might need to replace a bunny.

That was why he'd planned what he would do in this contingency. He'd picked out another suitable target ahead of time, making sure that he was able to take her whenever he needed to.

Of course, there were risks in such an action. Each time Frank acted openly increased the avenues through which someone might be able to find him. Each one gave a thread to pull on that might have him at its end. Frank hoped that his little reminder to Maya would be enough to stop her from pulling too hard, but it was impossible to know for sure.

There were dangers, but they felt like nothing compared to the prospect of leaving all of this incomplete. The prospect of that felt like a yawning chasm at the heart of him, threatening to devour everything Frank was. This was a great work that had to be fulfilled, had to be finished, or what was the point of beginning it at all?

No, he could not leave things as they were. His contingency plan would have to be put into motion.

Frank needed to catch another bunny for his collection.

CHAPTER FOUR

"So, let's go over all this again," Maya said, sitting across an interrogation room from the actor she'd saved.

A metal table stood between the two of them, and the chair on the suspect's side was bolted to the floor. The walls were plain gray, and a camera watched from the corner. The whole space was designed to create pressure on whoever was being interrogated, but right then, Maya wasn't sure that all that pressure would be necessary.

Harris was in there with her, looking as always like someone's rich uncle, in a suit Maya could never have hoped to afford, the stubble of his hair just starting to grow to the point where his bald spot was more obvious. The fact that the deputy director was even in the room told Maya just how seriously he was taking all this. Currently, he looked pretty frustrated. He'd obviously been hoping that they could bring in the kidnapper and end this. Even now, though, he had that hungry look in his eye that said he thought that there might be a way to keep closing the net.

"I've told you everything," the actor said. "I don't know what more you want."

"I want to see if there's anything else you remember when we go through it one more time," Maya said.

That wasn't the only reason, of course. Maya also wanted to see if there were any inconsistencies in his story that might point to a lie, to more that he wasn't saying. Repetition was important, and in this case, it might allow her to get to the truth of all of this.

"So your name is Brian Hessler?" Maya said. "And you're an unemployed actor. Is that right?"

"I get gigs," he replied, in a slightly hurt tone. He'd almost been killed and that was the part of this that bothered him?

"From kidnappers and killers," Harris put in from the side.

"I didn't know that at the time," Brian said. "I thought it was all a show!"

Maya nodded. "Yes, you've said that." She put in a deliberate note of disbelief into her voice so that he would feel as if he had to justify it. "How did you find out about this show?"

She could see how nervous the actor looked, starting to sweat slightly in the confines of the interview room.

"Their people got in touch with me through one of my online profiles. They said I was a natural for the role they had."

"A natural for the role of a kidnapper?" Harris said.

Brian looked even more uncomfortable at that. So far, he hadn't felt the need to lawyer up, but Maya got the feeling that he was starting to see just how much trouble he might be in. If he did get lawyers in, she had no doubt that they would advise him to cooperate in the hope of a deal.

"Was it *just* online messages?" Maya asked. Those would be hard to trace if the person who sent them knew what he was doing, and Maya had no doubt that the Moonlight Killer did.

"Of course not," Brian said. "There was a whole production team. A camera crew."

The Moonlight Killer had gone to a lot of trouble with all this, then, and somehow managed to do it all from behind the scenes. Maya had to believe that there would be *some* hint of evidence leading back to him, though.

"We'll need names for all of the production team," she said.

"I only really remember their first names," Brian said. "It was kind of a whirlwind, you know?"

Maya guessed that was deliberate, too. "And who was the person in charge?"

Was it possible that the Moonlight Killer was there? Had he been standing there in front of Brian, playing producer? Could Maya at least get a description of him? If so, then it would be one step closer to actually catching him.

"Well, the main money guy was some guy in crypto, paid everything in bitcoin," Brian said. "The producer was a woman. Maya something."

Maya had a horrible feeling about the next part of this. "Grey?"

Brian clicked his fingers. "That's it!"

He probably thought that he'd just helped her to uncover some key detail, rather than helping the Moonlight Killer to rub her face in the futility of trying to find him yet again.

Maya stood, feeling faintly sick. "I need to get some air."

She walked out of the interview room with Harris following her out into the bull pit. Around them, the other agents kept working their cases. The work of the department didn't stop just for this one case.

"This doesn't have to be a dead end," the deputy director said. "We can follow the money, track down the production company, find some trace of him."

Maya shook her head. "You know how unlikely all of that is, sir. You heard it yourself: he paid in crypto currency specifically to avoid a trail, and the production company will have vanished the moment he didn't need it to exist anymore."

"You make it sound like he's a ghost," Harris said. He clearly wasn't going to countenance the idea of someone able to stay out of the FBI's line of fire for long. Maybe he just didn't want to admit defeat.

"Not a ghost, just someone very, *very* clever, who's had more time to prepare than we have, and who is very careful not to leave traces."

"So we should just give up on trying to find him?" Harris said. It was obvious that he wasn't going to go along with that idea.

"I'm saying that we have to stop running into every trap he sets for us," Maya countered. "Do you think I don't want to catch this guy as much as you do? That I don't want him to pay for taking my sister, for making me play his little games? I want him, but I also want to be sure that when we go after him, we actually catch him. We need to be certain."

"At least we have his accomplice in there," Harris said. Even he didn't sound as if he really believed it.

"Accomplice?" Maya almost laughed. "He's a patsy. He thought he was taking part in a TV show. Maybe a jury will convict him of something, but he's not a part of this, and he certainly doesn't *know* anything."

Harris looked, if anything, even less happy. Probably because he knew that it was true.

"Ok, but I still want to take another run at him. Maybe I'll bring Reyes in, switch it up."

Maya was too tired to argue by then. "Yes, sir."

She watched Harris go back in, gesturing for Reyes to join him. Reyes, who was ambitious and driven, and who had made it clear from the start of this that he wanted to go straight ahead trying to catch the kidnapper. Maya let him go. On another day, she might have argued that this was her case, but for now, she was content for the two of them to try to get more out of Brian.

Maya went back to her desk. It was so frustrating. She wanted to scream out that frustration, but she couldn't exactly do that in the middle of the FBI's offices. She'd *told* Harris that a raid was a bad idea. Even her going in to scout had been a bad idea, but at the time, it had seemed like the only workable compromise.

She'd known that any approach would be seen by the Moonlight Killer as a breach of his rules. She'd been trying to make sure that they only went in if they were sure that it was him, and then she'd let herself get caught up in one more layer of the serial killer's tricks, because she'd thought she'd found a way to do it and still get away with it.

Maya needed to hear a friendly voice right then, and what did it say about her life that the only person she could think of who fit that definition was Marco Spinelli, the detective with whom she'd worked on murders in both Cleveland and Louisiana? What did it say that thoughts of Marco brought with them a warm feeling and the need to see him?

Maya called his number, waiting while it rang. When it went through to voicemail, Maya *did* curse aloud, and then had to endure the looks of her coworkers as they tried to work out if she was cursing because she'd had some kind of breakthrough in the case, or if she was suffering some sort of breakdown.

Maya remembered why she was calling, and spoke anyway.

"Hi, Marco, it's me. Just calling to check in, and see if you're ok. Things have been pretty weird here. My office thought they had another chance to catch the kidnapper. I managed to talk them into sending me in to scout, but it still turned into this whole raid on an empty building. I managed to pull one guy out, but he doesn't know anything. And the whole place got blown up, so there's no chance of forensics. Seriously, Marco, I don't know how they could all be so *stupid*."

She kept her voice low, making sure that no one else would hear, but she didn't hold back her frustration. Maya was doing everything she could, trying her best to keep everyone safe, but it felt as though her boss's decisions were undermining her at every turn. It felt impossible to make a difference when she couldn't really make any of the decisions about the case.

What if this time was the one that cost Megan her life? That was the fear that sat underneath the rest of it, eating away at her, threatening to overwhelm her while she sat here, waiting for Harris to try to find yet more ways to go after the Moonlight Killer.

It *might* be Megan. He'd already hurt her the last time Harris had insisted on a raid, and the only place for him to go to escalate from that was… just the thought of that made Maya shudder.

She realized that she was still on the phone to Marco's voicemail. "I'm sorry, I'm rambling. I'm ok. I just thought it would be good to hear your voice, but I know you're probably busy with your own cases. Maybe call me back when you have time."

Maya hung up and tried to think of something useful she could do instead of sitting there, fearing for her sister's life. Rather than chasing leads that the Moonlight Killer set up for them, Maya wanted to find something of her own.

The man sitting in their interrogation suite was one potential source of information, but he wasn't the only one, and he was a long way from the best option. There was still Katya Martin, the young woman the Moonlight Killer had released. She was still being checked over in the hospital, and Maya didn't want to go over there so soon, but there was still plenty she could do from here.

Maya started to look up Katya using the FBI's systems, finding her driver's license, her social media, everything that was out there to be found. Maya looked up her resume on the sites where she'd put it looking for work, and looked up her college records. She saw the life of a young woman who'd been going to college, had worked hard, had been moving on to the next phase of her life.

She started to look deeper, trying to find as many records as she could. She scanned the police reports that had come after Katya's disappearance, although there had been few enough of those. There hadn't been the concerted effort to find her that Maya might have expected in another case featuring some pretty young woman who'd suddenly gone missing.

That struck Maya as odd, so she tried to hunt for some kind of explanation.

Maya found the reason in one of the reports. Katya had been admitted to a series of psychiatric institutions in the course of her life. The reports weren't specific about the details of her condition, but it appeared to be some form of depression.

They hadn't searched for her, because they'd thought they were wasting their time. They'd assumed that she'd killed herself.

Maya found herself wondering about that, and about her sister. Megan had been off travelling and they'd lost touch. She'd been in a position where she wouldn't be missed, wouldn't be *found* for a long time. Was that the connection between them?

There was one interesting thing in the reports, though. Katya's last admission to a psych ward had been a couple of years ago, which wasn't what Maya might have expected. She'd been finishing the college courses that had been interrupted by her illness. She'd been moving on. Everyone had assumed that she'd relapsed and killed herself, but it looked as though that was anything but the case.

Or was Maya just thinking that because she'd found Katya? Because she knew that she hadn't killed herself? No one else had bothered looking for her, but Maya had found her. That was almost enough to give her one brief moment of hope to set against everything that had gone wrong in the last day or so.

Maya was sure that if she looked closely enough, if she got enough information, she would be able to find a link that would lead her to the Moonlight Killer. It was just a question of finding enough information, and she had leads. The tattoo on the Moonlight Killer's arm was one, while every woman released meant that they knew slightly more about him. If Maya saved enough of them, maybe she would actually be able to track him down.

If she did that, though, she wanted to be certain. She didn't want to walk into any more traps, didn't want to put any more women in danger.

Maya was still thinking about that when another of the agents there came over to her desk, holding a small box. Atop it sat the by now familiar shape of a postcard, this one featuring a rabbit with an injured paw, standing in the blown apart remains of a house.

"This just came in for you," the agent said. "No one saw it delivered."

Maya stared at the postcard with a kind of sick dread. The message was obvious: the Moonlight Killer had seen everything that happened at the house, and this was his response. Barely daring to do it, she opened the box.

A single human finger sat within.

CHAPTER FIVE

Detective Marco Spinelli kicked in the rear door of the small suburban house and immediately ducked back as a weapon spat bullets towards him.

"Cleveland PD!" he called out, as he tried to cram his tall, athletic frame into cover. "Give up now, and this doesn't have to get any worse."

More shots were his only answer, so Marco took out his own weapon and tried to work out where the perps were, ready to fire back. In the brief glance he got before he had to jerk his head back to avoid it being blown off, he saw a small, square kitchen, with a table tipped over onto its side, providing cover. The stove was on, with the smell burning steak starting to fill the air in the middle of the firefight.

"Give it up, Frankie," Marco called out. "You've got no way out of this."

Frankie Marsh, sometimes contract killer for one of Cleveland's crime families, didn't seem to agree. At least, he kept shooting. Marco kept his head down.

"You're the one who came here alone, cop," Marsh said. "I figure, I shoot you, then say you never identified yourself. Just some madman kicking in my door, I had to defend myself."

Marco had to admit that he had a point about that. He really should have brought backup for this one. He definitely shouldn't have come after a killer like Frankie Marsh alone. It was just that the only partner he'd been able to stand to work with in the last couple of years was currently in D.C., working cold cases at the whim of a madman.

"I have plenty of backup," Marco lied. "The whole front of the building is covered."

He heard Frankie laugh at that. He obviously didn't buy that for a second.

"Sure, let's pretend like that's true."

He wasn't firing off as many rounds now. It occurred to Marco that even a man like that might not have spare ammo on him at all times.

Maybe if Marco could make him waste that ammo, he might have a clear chance to get closer.

"How'd you even find me?" Marsh demanded, from behind the table. "Who gave me up?"

"Old man Vincenso himself," Marco said. It was another lie. He wasn't going to give away his real witnesses, wasn't going to risk them like that. But maybe if Frankie thought his boss was getting tired of him, there was a chance that he might flip and give Marco more. He found himself thinking that it was the kind of tactic that Maya might have employed. Probably, for her, it would have worked perfectly.

"You're lying," Frankie said. "He wouldn't sell me out."

"He would if he thought you'd become a liability," Marco said. He'd done enough work on gangs to know the kinds of reasons that people got given up. "The Adams murder was sloppy. You left evidence a blind man could have followed."

"I am never sloppy," Frankie said.

Sloppy enough to just admit to murder, but maybe that was just because he didn't expect Marco to live through this.

Marco considered his options. The first thing he did was to grab for his radio.

"This is Detective Spinelli, requesting backup to my location." he gave the address.

"I *knew* you didn't have any backup," Frankie said, and popped up to take a shot. He was a big man, solid from working out a lot, but also thick around the middle. Clearly too much time spent in this kitchen, waiting for the next job.

Marco let him drop back down, then considered the thickness of the table. One thing people always did was to underestimate just how easily bullets punched holes in objects. It took a lot more than a couple of inches of wood to slow one down.

Leaning out, Marco fired three times, straight through the table, aiming low.

"Shit!" Frankie swore, then came up, looking to fire. Marco could see the blood on his leg.

Marco's training urged him to put a couple of rounds into the center of mass. It was the hardest thing to miss, it put suspects down quickest, but the problem was that it would leave him with a dead perp on his hands and no chance of getting anything more. He didn't want to leave things like that. He didn't want the people who had ordered Frankie to make the hit to get away with it.

So he shot the contract killer in the shoulder instead.

The impact didn't send him flying, because that was something that only happened in the movies. Instead, Frankie's gun went off in almost the same moment, slamming a bullet into the wall beside Marco. For a moment, Marco's breath caught as he realized just how close that had been, but there was no time to focus on that, because Frankie's gun was falling to the ground from nerveless fingers.

Marco charged forward, his body weight slamming into the hitman, knocking him off his feet. Frankie was big, but Marco was at least as tall, with the lean muscles of a swimmer. Combine that with the killer's injured leg, and there was no way he could stay standing.

Marco kicked away Frankie's gun, keeping his own weapon trained on him the whole time.

"Don't move, Frankie. You're under arrest."

Even like that, the hitman tried to kick out at him, so that Marco had to wrestle him over onto his stomach and cuff him. It was only as he did so that he heard the sirens outside. It seemed that his backup had arrived.

*

"Well done on the arrest," Chief Linden said, as the two of them stood in his office back at the station. "Maybe with one of their main killers behind bars, we'll have a way through to the rest of the operation."

Chief Linden was a solidly built man who always kept his uniform immaculate, so that there was no chance of him looking untidy at a press conference.

"Maybe," Marco said. Personally, he doubted it. He suspected that Frankie was going to clam up completely, and that if he didn't then he would quickly find himself killed, police custody or not. Solving one crime didn't mean that the whole house of cards was going to come falling down. Not without a lot more evidence.

That was a frustrating feeling. Knowing that Frankie wouldn't talk, or would simply be killed, meant that Marco had been in real danger today, and for what? He didn't feel as though he was making a difference.

"You have to learn to celebrate moments like this," Chief Linden insisted. "You've been doing good work, Spinelli."

Marco suspected that there was a "but" coming. Chief Linden could be effusive with his praise when there were cameras watching, but he had rarely been Marco's biggest fan in private.

"Although I'm a little worried that you went into such a dangerous situation alone. I think it's time we talked about you having a partner again."

There it was. Marco didn't want another partner; or at least, he didn't want any of the ones who would come out of the detective pool at the station. There was only one person in the last few years he'd truly enjoyed working with, and she was back in D.C.

"We've had this conversation before," Marco said.

Chief Linden shrugged. "We have, but this time, I'm not taking no for an answer. This case is too important to risk leaving it with just one cop. If we're going to break up the crime families, then I can't have situations where we might lose you in the middle of the investigation."

"This is my case," Marco said. Even if it didn't feel as if today made a difference, he still wasn't going to just let this go.

"And now it can be yours and a partner's," Chief Linden said. "Or I'll reassign the whole thing to other detectives. Ones who know how to work as a team."

"We'll talk, sir," Marco said, trying to hide his frustration. "But I'd better get on with the paperwork for all of this. It doesn't do itself."

It was better to deflect attention than to confront his boss head on, and there was little that deflected Chief Linden's attention quite as effectively as paperwork.

"True, true," Chief Linden said.

Marco went back to his desk, piled high with potential cases. You could say this for life in Cleveland: it wasn't as though a detective ever ran out of things to do. He'd made an arrest in one murder, but there were more waiting, and plenty of other serious crimes stacked along with them if he somehow managed to get through those.

He should have been too busy to do anything other than dive into the next case, but for now, at least, he took a moment to breathe. Marco got out his phone and checked to see if he'd missed anything while he'd been busy chasing after a killer.

When he saw that there was a voicemail from Maya's number, Marco felt his heart starting to beat faster just at the sight of her name. Every thought of her did, at the moment. Yes, their one attempt at a date had ended with her drunk and talking too much about work, and him feeling as if he was just there to be a sounding board for her, but Marco was more than willing to put up with that if it meant getting to see her.

He guessed that this message would be something about her case, but even so, Marco sat and listened, wanting to hear all of it.

"Hi, Marco, it's me. Just calling to check in, and see if you're ok. Things have been pretty weird here. My office thought they had another chance to catch the kidnapper. I managed to talk them into sending me in to scout, but it still turned into this whole raid on an empty building. I managed to pull one guy out, but he doesn't know anything. And the whole place got blown up, so there's no chance of forensics. Seriously, Marco, I don't know how they could all be so *stupid*."

Marco could hear the mixture of emotions in her voice: the anger, the frustration, the worry. Surprisingly, the one emotion that he *couldn't* hear there was fear. That was both impressive and worrying. It reinforced how tough, how capable Maya was that she didn't sound as though she was shaking so soon after what sounded like a pretty close call. At the same time, though, it worried Marco that she could almost be blown up, and she was talking about it like the most difficult part was the one where a suspect wouldn't give her answers.

Was her need to get answers pushing her into places where she might be in danger?

The thought of Maya nearly being hurt brought out the need to speak with her, to see her. It had been a week or more since Marco had last seen Maya, and in spite of the brief time that they'd known one another Marco found that he missed having her around more than he could have imagined.

Listening to the message again, he got the feeling that she needed him there, too. As far as he knew, he was the only other person who knew the full truth of what was going on with the kidnappings: that Maya's sister was in the hands of the Moonlight Killer, not some random guy. It was more than that, though. Marco could see the ways in which Maya was spiraling down into all of this, getting more and more caught up in it all, more willing to take risks or do things that he suspected that she might never have done before.

It was only a matter of time before that got her hurt, or worse. It could lead to her getting too close and not being willing to take in backup, so that it was her facing up to a killer alone. She was being drawn in more and more, and Marco was sure Maya thought it was her making progress, but what if this was all some big web with a spider waiting at its heart?

Marco wasn't sure how long he'd been thinking about all of this. Not just today, not just since the message, that was certain. Maybe since the moment he'd met Maya, or since he'd gone to help her in Louisiana, learning just how important it was for her to have someone around who could remind her to come up for air once in a while, and who could stop her from going too far in all of this.

However long it had been, he'd come to a decision now. She needed someone there beside her, someone there who could keep her safe and maybe even hold her back from all the things she might do if she thought it was the only way to get to the Moonlight Killer.

Marco needed to be that someone. He needed to be there for her. He *wanted* to be there for her, and there wasn't anyone else who could do it. He'd found out the hard way, though, that there was no way of doing it from Cleveland. He had to be there with her, if he was going to help her.

Doing that meant one thing. Marco couldn't put this off any longer. He stood and walked over to Chief Linden's office, knocking on the door.

"What is it, Spinelli? Did your hitman crack already?"

"I want to request a transfer, sir," Marco said. "Ideally, I'd like you to talk to Deputy Director Harris of the FBI cold cases unit and have me attached there, but failing that, anywhere in D.C."

Chief Linden gave him a shocked look, staring as if he couldn't quite believe what he'd heard. Marco watched as he tried to put the pieces together.

"This is about Agent Grey, I take it?" Linden said, after several seconds. "You get the hots for one agent, and now you want to go running off across the country to be near her?"

He made it sound as though it was nothing, some stupid notion.

“This isn’t just about Maya, sir,” Marco said, although she was by far the biggest part of it. “I want to feel as though I’m doing something that matters, and this case definitely does.”

“So do all the ones waiting on your desk,” Chief Linden shot back, sounding angry now. He shook his head. “Request denied.”

On another day, maybe Marco would have let it go, but today, he’d been shot at, nearly killed, and it hadn’t been enough to make a real difference.

“I’m sorry sir, but that’s not good enough,” Marco said. He turned and headed for the door.

“Where are you going, Spinelli?”

Marco didn’t look back at his boss. Instead, he strode towards the door to the office.

“You can call it a leave of absence, or you can call it me quitting. It’s your choice, sir.”

Either way, he had to get to Maya to help her with all of this. Marco didn’t know how much danger she was going to be in without him, but he was pretty sure that the sooner he got to her, the better.

CHAPTER SIX

For the longest time, Maya could only sit at her desk and stare at the finger in silent horror.

She'd seen worse before in her life. Of course, she'd seen worse. She'd been to war. She'd seen death and destruction in all its forms. She'd seen people reduced to fragments by IEDs, ripped apart in the worst possible ways. Even now, she dealt with death as a normal part of her job. She should have been used to it.

Yet there was something about that single finger sitting there that was worse. Something that seemed to cut through to the heart of her just by being there. It took Maya what seemed like forever to work out what the difference was:

This was her fault.

Her fault. Those words seemed to echo through her, finding a deep pit of guilt that couldn't be filled.

It wasn't just her fault, though, and that thought was enough to propel her up out of her seat, taking the box with the finger in it and the postcard over to Harris's office. Maya knocked perfunctorily, but walked in without waiting to be invited.

Harris looked up as she entered, and something of Maya's anger must have shown on her face, because she could see him building up to tell her to cool off.

That faded away almost instantly when she put the box down on his desk.

"Is that-"

"A woman's finger? Yes," Maya didn't even try to keep the way she felt out of her voice. "The kidnapper did this because of us trying to find him."

"We're going to have this conversation again?" Harris asked. He obviously wasn't going to take that kind of condemnation from someone who worked for him, yet Maya needed him to understand the stakes.

"I just need you to understand how dangerous this man is," she said.

“A vigilante who wants to catch the Moonlight Killer should be no match for the FBI,” Harris insisted.

Even so, he didn’t sound as confident as usual. Maya caught his eyes flicking down towards the finger.

“Yes, he is.” Maya shook her head. “He’s constantly ahead of us. And the latest postcard? ‘Do not disappoint me again’? He’s saying that it’s our final warning. I’m listening to that, but that doesn’t make any difference if *you* don’t listen.”

Maya turned the postcard so that Harris could read it. She watched the deputy director scan it carefully, wincing at the contents. She saw the moment when a puzzled look came over his face.

“Is Christine Weller the name of the woman he did this to, or…”

“Another case,” Maya said. “At least, I assume so. I haven’t had any time to check the details yet.”

Harris did not look happy about that, either. “He does this, and in the same breath expects us to go running around, doing his bidding again?”

Maya could understand *that* feeling, at least. It was one that she shared. She didn’t like being at the beck and call of the Moonlight Killer any more than Harris did. Possibly less, since she knew exactly who she was dealing with, while Harris still thought that it was some kidnapper with a grudge against the killer.

“It’s a reminder of exactly what he’s capable of if we *don’t* do what he wants,” Maya said to her boss. That was the part of this that hadn’t changed. One week from now, if she didn’t find a murderer, then a young woman was going to die.

“That’s true.” Harris was staring down at the box again. “I suppose we owe it to this young woman to try to save her now. We did this much to her. Maybe we can save the rest of her.”

Maya hadn’t heard her boss accept responsibility for what had happened to the women before. He’d always been so adamant that it had been solely a choice of the kidnapper. Maybe he was starting to understand that, in spite of the resources of the FBI, they didn’t have all the power in this situation.

Maya hoped that he was starting to understand, because it was the only way that her sister was going to stay alive long enough for Maya to save her. If Harris kept charging in trying to catch the Moonlight Killer, then Megan was going to die.

“There is one… worrying aspect to all of this, though,” Harris said.

"More worrying than the fact that a psychopath has my sister and seven other women as his prisoner?" Maya countered, unable to stop herself.

Harris was stony faced. "He has killed two of the people we identified as being responsible for the murders. Is this the same vigilante instinct that has him going after the Moonlight Killer? If so, will he attempt to kill every murderer you uncover?"

"As far as I know, Kyle, the kid who killed Anne Postmartin, is alive and well," Maya pointed out, although she had also wondered why that was.

"Perhaps because he showed some contrition?" Harris suggested.

"Maybe," Maya replied, although that didn't seem like the kind of thing that would make much of a difference to the Moonlight Killer. It was probably more relevant that Kyle hadn't gone into it trying to make the murder look like the serial killer's work. People had assumed that it was the Moonlight Killer, but he hadn't actively tried to pass his own work off as that of the serial killer. "We *are* sure that he's ok?"

"I haven't had any word from the correctional facility he's in, but I'll check," Harris said. "You see the problem though, Grey? Are we merely helping a killer to identify his next victims? And if we are, can we justify it, even to keep the hostages safe?"

Was Harris saying that he might not send her out on this after all? Maya couldn't allow that. She had to do everything in her power to get on this and solve this. Her sister's life hung in the balance.

"I think that the men he's targeting are all murderers," Maya said.

"So they deserve it?"

"More than the women he's kidnapped?" Maya didn't answer that, because her boss already knew what she was saying. Besides, there were far more convincing arguments. "In any case, we know that with at least one of the killers, he *knew* who it was, because he was able to give me clues. If he already knows, then failing to solve the murders won't do anything to keep these people safe, it will just put the women he's holding at risk. If you want to protect the killers from him, it may be that the only way to do it is to identify them and then hope that our protection is up to the job."

Maya knew that she had her boss there, and it seemed that he did too. He didn't look happy about it, though.

“Very well, but we need to tread carefully with this. I don’t like the fact that this bastard thinks he can swoop in and kill our prisoners whenever he wants.”

The problem was that, so far, he *had* been able to. He, or people sent by him, had been able to get to prisoners who should have been safely held in custody. Maya shrugged. That part wasn’t down to her. It was for the corrections service or the US Marshals to deal with.

Her business was making sure that they caught whoever this was in the first place. It was finding answers, before the Moonlight Killer’s deadline ran out.

“I need to look up the case,” Maya said. They didn’t have an address this time, just a name.

“There could be a dozen Christine Wellers who have been killed over the years.”

It was possible, but even if there were, Maya knew exactly which case it would be: whichever one had been mistaken for the Moonlight Killer. That was the point of it, what her sister’s captor was trying to achieve. Maya went back to her desk, opened her computer, and tapped in the name.

It wasn’t hard to find the possibility she wanted. Christine Weller, a teacher in the small town of Hastel, New Hampshire. Even the briefest glance at the newspaper reports showed the fear that the Moonlight Killer had struck there. The strangest thing was how recent it all was: just three months ago. For a cold case, that was still pretty warm.

Maya looked at the reports and realized how easy it would be to spend the next week simply reading through them all, trying to catch up with everything that was being said about the case. When people thought that a serial killer had struck in a town that small, it meant more pages of newsprint and reports than Maya could hope to go through and still do her job. In the last few cases, though, the answer hadn’t been in the reports; it had been there, on the ground, in the towns where the killings had taken place.

Maya didn’t want to wade through all of the Moonlight Killer stuff when she was pretty sure that none of it would be relevant. She already knew that the *real* Moonlight Killer was the one sending her on these cases, and that he was doing it specifically so that Maya would show that he hadn’t been the one to do any of them.

Apparently, the serial killer cared about making sure that he only got credit for his own crimes. Maya still wasn’t sure why that was.

Perhaps some grandiose sense that the others were cheap imitators? She half-suspected that understanding the reason might be another way to try to inch her way closer to catching him. Right now, though, she didn't have any time for that, only to get moving and try to get a head-start on this case.

She looked around until she found Reyes. "Reyes? You want to be a part of all this?"

"I *am* a part of it," Reyes retorted. "You're not a one-woman agency."

"Then do me a favor and go through everything on the Weller case. Call me with the highlights."

"And what will you be doing in the meantime?" Reyes asked, sounding suspicious. He'd obviously guessed that Maya was using him.

Maya shrugged. It should have been obvious. "I'll be heading to New Hampshire, trying to solve a murder."

She kept a travel bag at work now, tucked into the bottom of her desk, with a few clothes ready to go. She threw in her tactical vest and her laptop. She could book a flight on the way to the airport, using her phone.

And was halfway through trying to find a hotel to stay at when Marco's number flashed up on her screen as he called her.

Maya answered instantly. Even in the middle of all of this, she wasn't going to make him wait, and she was all too aware of the ways she'd ignored him over the last few weeks, only getting in contact when she needed something.

"Hey, Marco." In spite of everything that had happened in the last day or so, the warmth in Maya's voice was genuine.

"Is this a good time?" Marco asked.

"I have a couple of minutes," Maya said. "Then I have to go catch a flight. Another postcard arrived."

"Another one? After the raid?" There was a pause for a second or two as Marco thought. "He isn't sending you to find another body, is he?"

Maya felt grateful to be talking to someone who actually understood how bad it could be.

"No, he already gave us his sick idea of a punishment by sending us a woman's finger."

"A *finger*?" Marco sounded shocked by it, but he seemed to recover quickly. "I want to come up to D.C. and help you with all of this. Can I meet you at your flight?"

Marco wanted to come help her with all of this? That meant more to Maya than she could say, after the way she'd more or less ignored him in her past case. There was no one she would rather work on all this with than him. If he could do it, then she definitely wasn't going to turn down the help.

Harris would probably be okay with it, after the times Marco had helped in the past. Right then, though, Maya didn't care.

"Are you sure? After last time-"

"I'm sure," Marco said. "I can't just sit here in Cleveland while I know that this is going on. While you're having to deal with it all alone."

Maya wasn't sure how to thank him for that. The hardest part of it was being the only one who knew the full truth, having no one she could talk to about any of it.

"Like I said, I'm taking a flight, to New Hampshire," Maya said. "I'm trying to get to a town called Hastel."

"I can meet you there?" Marco suggested.

"If you're sure?"

"I'm sure."

Maya was amazed that the detective was willing to go to this much trouble for her. Before, he'd had cases to work on, and had made it clear that he had to focus on them. Now he was doing this?

Maya wasn't about to turn down help, though, especially not when it came from him.

"I'd like that," Maya said. "I'll meet you at the police precinct there?"

"Sounds good to me. I'd better go book a flight."

"Same here," Maya said. She didn't want to just hang up, but neither of them had any time right then. "And Marco? Thank you for all this. It means a lot."

With him there, she wouldn't have to deal with all this alone. With him there, she had the backup she needed. Maybe, just maybe, it would be enough to catch the killer in time.

For now, though, she had to get to New Hampshire. She had a killer to catch, before it cost another woman her life.

CHAPTER SEVEN

Welcome to Hastel, the Boardgame Capital of America, Maya read as she drove past, along a highway that led in between neat rows of houses. Maya guessed it was a better thing for a town to focus on than the murder in its midst.

Unfortunately, her focus had to be on finding a killer, not on anything as peaceful and simple as boardgames. The town was bigger than she thought, with plenty of brightly painted buildings, almost as if someone had decided that they should live up to the sign by looking like the pieces from some kind of game themselves.

Even the street names got in on the act. Maya didn't notice it at first, because her family get togethers hadn't been the kind where they sat around and played games together, but even she got the message when she saw Clue Avenue and Monopoly Boulevard, one after another.

She found the police department a couple of streets after that, and even it seemed to want to get in on the town's schtick, since the sign outside it read *Hastel Police Department (Do not pass go).*

Maya got the feeling that the kind of tourists the town attracted probably loved that. Maybe they had their photographs taken in front of it. She just hoped that things were a little more serious inside.

Marco was waiting out in front of the building, standing there looking slightly disheveled, but every bit as good as Maya remembered him. He was tall, clean shaven, with dark hair that never looked as though it had been properly tamed by a comb. He had the tapered body of an athlete, with the most piercing blue-gray eyes Maya had seen. Currently he was wearing slacks, a plaid shirt and a waxed cotton jacket. His smile had even more warmth in it than Maya remembered.

"It's good to see you," Maya said, and that barely covered any of what she was feeling in that moment. A part of her wanted to just hug him, but she wasn't sure if that was the best thing to be seen to do outside a police station she was about to walk into and assert her authority as an agent reinvestigating a case.

She wasn't even sure if it was the right thing to do, given how complicated things had gotten between them so quickly.

"You too," Marco replied, and Maya got the feeling that he was holding back almost as much as she was. "What are we dealing with here?"

"The death of a woman called Christine Weller. She was killed about four months ago, and people assumed it was the Moonlight Killer."

"But we know that it can't be him," Marco said.

That was one of the best things about having him there: he got this. He was the only other person, right now, who knew exactly what was going on with the kidnappings.

It was just one of the reasons that Maya was glad to have him there. It also helped that he was a good detective, and having him around would make it easier to go through whatever evidence there was for this case.

Then there was just the fact that it was *him,* and having Marco close by seemed to make everything a little brighter. It certainly made Maya's heart beat a little faster in her chest.

"We know that," Maya said. "But we still have to find out who actually did it. Which reminds me…"

She took out her phone and set it on loudspeaker as she called Reyes.

"Grey."

"You've been through the files?" Maya asked.

"What there is of them. There are more newspaper reports than anything. People are pretty convinced that it was the Moonlight Killer this time."

"We'll see," Maya replied. She couldn't let on yet that she already knew it wasn't the prolific serial killer, because that would lead to questions about how she knew, and Maya didn't want to let slip the fact that she'd been holding back evidence. "What do you have on the victim?"

"Christine Weller, 32 years old, lived at 24 Catan Place. Is that really a street name? Like the board game?"

"You should see this place," Maya said. Even the graffiti on a wall across the street was of a game board. "Keep going."

"She was killed on the 23rd of April, at night, while the moon was out, strangled with a rope and left outside her own home. Nothing taken and no sign of a break in."

Which ruled out some of the simpler possibilities, such as a robbery gone wrong.

"What about her life?" Maya asked.

"She was a teacher. Had a boyfriend called Brent Miles."

"I take it someone looked at the boyfriend," Marco said.

"Who's that?" Reyes asked.

"Detective Spinelli is here." Maya didn't feel as though she owed Reyes more of an explanation than that. "He's going to be assisting with this case."

"If you wanted backup, I'm sure Harris would have sent me with you," Reyes pointed out.

That was the last thing that Maya wanted. Reyes charged into things too quickly, assumed that he was in charge, and was more interested in working his way up the ladder of promotion than actually getting things *right*.

"You're needed there. Marco can help. He's helped before. Now, *did* anyone look at Christine Weller's boyfriend?"

Maya waited, presumably while Reyes dug up the relevant part of the file.

"He had an alibi. He was out with a couple of guys from work at a bar called McCabe's, got drunk, then crashed on one of their floors."

Meaning that he hadn't been anywhere near the house when his girlfriend had been murdered. Maya guessed that hearing about it like this was better than wasting time chasing a dead end.

"Ok, thanks, Reyes," Maya said. "Harris has arranged everything with the local PD?"

After the welcome she'd received on at least one previous case, Maya wanted to make sure that the way was clear for her.

"They're waiting for you."

"Great." Maya hung up. She looked over at Marco. "Ready to go in?"

He nodded and the two of them went into the police station together, into a reception area that seemed to have been randomly decorated with artwork in the shape of gaming pieces. Was this meant to be a police station or a tourist attraction?

Maya walked up to the reception desk and showed her badge to the middle-aged woman behind it.

"Agent Grey, FBI. This is Detective Spinelli, who is working as a consultant with me. My boss called ahead."

Maya decided that it was important to introduce Marco like that, so that there wouldn't be any questions about why a detective from Cleveland was there.

The receptionist nodded and gestured to a side door. "Detective Simms is waiting for you. If you want to wait through there, I'll call him down."

Maya went through the side door and was slightly disappointed to find that it was an interview room with a single table in the middle and chairs set on either side.

"They're treating us more like witnesses or perps than cops," Marco said.

"It's just the usual thing of wanting to show the FBI that this is their town." Maya was more than used to it by now. "We just have to hope that they're not going to be like the ones in Pollock."

Maya didn't want more resistance, even outright sabotage, the way she'd experienced from Sheriff Recks there. With how difficult these cases could be, Maya needed all the assistance that she could get.

Maya was still considering that when a cop walked in. He was short, bald, and so overweight that her first impression was of a cannonball in a suit, almost waddling in with a coffee in one hand and a manila file in the other.

"Detective Simms?" Maya asked.

"That's me. You must be Agent Grey, and this is?"

"Detective Spinelli, Cleveland PD," Maya said. "He's consulting with me on this."

"An agent *and* a consultant," Detective Simms said, in a jovial tone. "It seems as though you're taking all this pretty seriously."

"Murder seems worth taking seriously," Maya pointed out. Was the last comment a sign that the local police department hadn't given the investigation their full efforts? For the purposes of her investigation, it was probably a good thing. The most terrifying thing would be if she showed up to an investigation and found that everything had been examined perfectly, with no hint of additional information to be found.

Would the Moonlight Killer do that to her? Would he deliberately set her an impossible case?

Maya had to believe that he wouldn't. He wanted these cases solved. If it was impossible to do so, then why bother sending her in the first place?

"Oh, we took it very seriously," Detective Simms assured her. "We checked every aspect of Christine Weller's life, but there was nothing there to find. Frankly, it didn't make sense that anyone would want to kill her."

"No enemies?" Marco said. Maya caught the slight note of disbelief there. Given the gang cases he'd worked back in Cleveland, maybe he had a hard time believing that anyone could have no enemies.

Detective Simms shook his head. He opened up the file he held. "Not one. She was the teacher everyone loved. There were no former pupils with a grudge, no parents upset that their kid wasn't getting attention. There was nothing on her social media accounts, and no sign of any threatening messages in the weeks leading up to all of this. She didn't owe anyone money, and there were no obvious secrets that someone might have killed her over. We briefly looked at her boyfriend, but he had an alibi."

Detective Simms closed the file with a snap. Maya could see the look of satisfaction on his face as he did it. He was obviously making it clear that his department had gone over all the ground that Maya might possibly want to cover.

"So that was the point when you decided that it had to be the Moonlight Killer?" Maya asked.

She saw Detective Simms shrug. "We couldn't work out what else it could be. She was killed on April 23rd, the full moon, strangled and left. What part of that doesn't fit the Moonlight Killer?"

Maya had to admit that it sounded pretty consistent, yet she and Marco both knew that it couldn't be. She knew that this wasn't the Moonlight Killer, but she suspected that simply telling that to the detective in front of her wouldn't be enough.

"I've heard about you," Detective Simms said. "As soon as I heard you were coming, I looked you up. It looks as though you've spent the last few weeks finding other killers in old cases that were attributed to the Moonlight Killer."

"I'm just interested in finding whoever did this," Maya said.

"I'm telling you though, we were thorough. This one is the serial killer. I don't know what you think you can do that can prove otherwise."

One thought came to her. Something sounded wrong about April 23rd. Maya had spent plenty of time looking at the Moonlight Killer's cases, and one aspect of them felt as though it had crept under her skin. The phases of the moon were embedded on the edges of her consciousness now, and something about the date felt… off.

Getting out her phone, Maya looked it up.

"Am I boring you, Agent?" Detective Simms asked.

"Sorry, just checking something."

"You've found something?" Marco asked. His tone was a lot less skeptical than Detective Simms's, but then, he knew her a lot better.

"I was just checking the phases of the moon," Maya said. She turned her screen so that Detective Simms could see it. "April 23rd was the day *before* the full moon. Close enough for someone playing copycat, but not for the Moonlight Killer. Trust me, he gets the date of the full moon *right*."

Maya saw the realization that he was wrong spreading across Detective Simms's face.

"That can't be right. Something like that…"

"You wouldn't have thought to check," Maya said. "You could see the moon. It looked close enough to full. But I've spent enough time looking at the Moonlight Killer's cases that I *know* when the full moon is by now."

"It could still be him," Detective Simms insisted. "He could have varied his pattern, or gotten it wrong."

Maya gave him a level look. "How likely do you really think either of those things is?"

Detective Simms sat there for a moment or two and then shook his head sharply. He didn't look happy about it.

"You know what this means, though?" he said.

Maya nodded. "I know. It means that you have a killer still out there somewhere in your community. One who is sure they have gotten away with it. I intend to prove them wrong on that."

"We'll give you any resources you require," Detective Simms said. "We'll find an office for you, and if you need anything else, let me know. Where are you planning to start?"

Maya was planning on starting in the place she always started with these crimes, in the one spot where everything had changed, and a life had ended.

"I want to take a look around the crime scene. Maybe I'll see something there that will help."

CHAPTER EIGHT

Maya wasn't sure what she expected from 24 Catan Place. It sat on a broad, tree lined avenue, with wooden built houses on either side that were almost identical to one another. There was another one of those game piece statues at the end of the street, and Maya found herself realizing just how seriously the town took its reputation as the boardgame capital of the country.

Maya didn't think the house was particularly large, but then, why would it be on a teacher's salary? There were real estate signs up in front of it at the moment, and Maya realized that for once, she was close enough to the time a crime had happened that she was still seeing the aftermath. Probably, Christine's family hadn't finished dealing with all her affairs even now. Selling a house where a murder had taken place couldn't be easy.

"What are you expecting to see?" Marco asked as they pulled up. He was driving, leaving Maya free to look the street over as they approached. It was quiet, the sounds of the city muffled by the trees.

"I'm not expecting anything," Maya said. They parked on the street outside the house and got out, looking around. "I just want to get a sense of how it all happened."

Maya got out and started looking around, taking in the bushes around the edge of the driveway, and the low wall running between one property and the next. There was a passage that presumably led through to a back yard, running between the main house and a separate garage.

Each one of those looked to Maya like a spot where it might have been possible to ambush someone.

She was still looking when she saw a neighbor come out of a house across the street: an older woman in workout clothes who looked as though she might be about to head out for a run.

"Oh, are you thinking of moving to the neighborhood?" the woman called out. "It's a lovely place."

"I'm sure it is," Maya said, letting her go off about her run. She added the presence of neighbors to the picture she was already starting to build of the crime scene.

She could see Marco looking the building over, just as she was.

"Why attack outside?" Maya asked. "Does that rule out someone she knew?"

"Maybe, or maybe they were just trying to be sure it wasn't obviously them," Marco suggested. "Killing someone so close to the full moon suggests that they were at least *trying* to confuse things."

"If they did that part deliberately."

After all, if they were truly trying to copy the Moonlight Killer, wouldn't they have checked the date of the full moon first? Was that part just a coincidence? Was it something the police had simply latched onto to make their lives simpler?

Maya tried to imagine what it would have been like for Christine, coming home that night, maybe hearing someone behind her, probably trying to get to her front door and get inside.

Then feeling the rope slip around her neck. She wouldn't have been able to cry out at that point, and in the dark, with the bushes surrounding everything, her neighbors wouldn't have even had a chance to see her struggling with her murderer.

"Do you want to see if we can get access inside?" Marco asked. "It shouldn't be hard, if they're selling the place."

Maya shook her head, though. "It happened here, and I think we can rule out anything random. To kill her here, the killer would have had to lie in wait. He chose his hiding spot and he struck when she got close to her door."

"Always the most dangerous time," Marco agreed.

He had a point. People on the move were harder to attack. The dangerous moments were the moments of transition, where they had to stop and give their attention to things like getting out the correct key. The killer here had done this quickly and expertly. He'd planned it as carefully as a commander might have planned a military ambush.

Which meant that somewhere, there was someone who hated Christine Weller enough to sit down and decide to kill her, whatever the local police thought.

"Where now?" Marco asked. He looked as though he wanted to scour every inch of the place for evidence, but four months on, there was no chance of finding anything new.

"Now, we go to talk to Christine Weller's family."

*

As Maya approached the address, she saw that this house was bigger, obviously built with a family in mind. It looked like the kind of place that might once have had a neatly kept front lawn and everything kept pristine, yet it was obvious that no one had done much work around it in a few months. There were a couple of cars on the driveway.

"This is the place," Maya said. "And it looks as though they're home."

"Should we have called ahead?" Marco asked her.

It was a reasonable point, but Maya wanted an honest reaction from Christine's family. She wanted to see what they really felt and thought, not what they'd composed themselves to say in the time it took to get there. With the limited time that Maya had on this case, she had to move quickly.

"It will be fine," Maya assured him.

"Just remember that this case is a lot fresher than most of the ones you work," Marco said. "Emotions will still be raw."

"That pain doesn't go away just because time passes." Maya had seen plenty of families where the pain of losing a loved one had never truly left. Her own pain at Megan being in the Moonlight Killer's hands wasn't going to leave her anytime soon either. "I'll be careful."

She walked up to the door and rang the bell. A man in his fifties answered it. He looked as though he might once have been fit and quite good looking, but now he just looked drained, as though everything had been taken out of him, all at once. His dark hair looked unkempt, and Maya doubted that he'd changed his clothes in a few days. He looked pallid, and when he spoke, it was as if he could barely summon up the strength to talk.

"Yes? If you're more reporters-"

"I'm Maya Grey, with the FBI." Maya showed him her ID. "This is Detective Marco Spinelli. We're reinvestigating your daughter's death, hoping to find new leads. May we come in?"

The man looked at them for what seemed like an eternity before he nodded. "Yes, anything, if it will help to catch the person who did this."

He showed them into a hallway that had family pictures running along one wall.

"Jason, who is it?"

"It's the FBI, Sinead."

He led the way through to a living room where the drapes were half closed even though it was the middle of the day. Two women sat there on a large sofa. One was roughly the same age as the man, with long dark hair, looking as if she hadn't eaten properly in a while, with dark rings under her eyes. The other was probably in her mid-to-late twenties, her hair cut short, wearing jeans and a scarlet sweatshirt.

"You're with the FBI?" the younger woman asked, as if she didn't quite believe it. Maybe she thought that they were reporters lying to get access to the family.

Maya held out her ID for her to look at. "I am. Marco here is a detective who's consulting with me on this case."

She didn't mention the other cases that she'd worked on recently. Ultimately, why would this family care about any grief but their own right then?

"You're Christine's sister?" Maya guessed.

"Dina," the younger woman said. "Christine used to joke that if you said our names too close together, it sounded like an echo."

It was the kind of small thing that probably hurt to remember, now that her sister was gone. Marco had been right; the feelings here were still going to be very raw.

Jason Weller gestured for them to sit down in a pair of large armchairs. Maya perched on the edge of hers, leaning forward. It felt strange to intrude on such recent grief like this, but ultimately, she knew that she had to do it if she was going to find answers in this case. The only way of giving this family closure was to ask her questions, find out about Christine.

"So the FBI is here because of the Moonlight Killer angle?" Dina asked.

Maya shook her head. "Actually, no. I'm not sure that the Moonlight Killer did this."

She could have been more definitive than that, but if she had been and it got back to Harris, she would have to explain exactly why she was so certain, so quickly.

She saw the shock there on the face of Sinead Weller, offset by a kind of deep relief on the features of Jason Weller.

"You think that it was someone else?" Christine's mother said. "But we were told… I was so certain… I thought it was him."

"That's understandable," Maya said. "Everyone seems to have thought so, but the facts of the case just don't fit the Moonlight Killer's

MO. I'm here because I work on cold cases, and because I believe there's a chance that if I go through things with a fresh pair of eyes, I might be able to find the person who actually did this."

"But after so long, it must be almost impossible," Sinead said. "Have the police wasted all this time chasing after the wrong thing?"

"At least this means that my baby wasn't preyed on by some kind of serial killer," Jason Weller said.

Maya wasn't sure if that really made things better or worse. It didn't bring back his daughter, but on the other hand, maybe it meant that he might actually see some kind of justice done for her death.

It definitely would if Maya had anything to do with this, and not just because it was the only way to save another woman's life. The family deserved everything she could do to help them.

"Maya is good," Marco said. "I've seen her find answers in cases that seemed as though they were impossible. But we need you to tell us more about Christine. We need to know about her and her life."

There was a warmth to the way he said it that seemed to put the Wellers at ease. Maya could see Sinead Weller's expression shift to something more determined.

"Yes, of course, anything you need."

"Christine was a teacher?" Maya said. Was it possible that her job might have something to do with this?

"Yes, that's right. Up at the local high school."

"Did she ever have any problems in her job? Any arguments with colleagues? Any problem students she had to deal with?"

Jason Weller answered that one. "Christine never had any problems with anyone. She was a wonderful teacher, and she always found a way to help her students. When she died, there were so many messages of support from them all. I think they were almost as heartbroken as we were."

Maya looked over to Dina. "Did your sister mention anyone she had any trouble with? Maybe something that she wouldn't want to tell your parents?"

"No, she always seemed to like her colleagues," Dina said. "I'd try to do the sister thing of getting her to complain about work, but Christine loved the school. She felt as though she was making a difference with her work. I… I guess you know about that."

Most days, Maya would have said yes, but just recently, it felt as though she was caught up in something she couldn't escape. Something where no number of right answers would be enough to keep her sister safe. It felt as though she was only just staying ahead of the Moonlight Killer's demands, and if she put a foot wrong, then the consequences could be disastrous.

She had to focus, though, if she was going to solve this.

"What about her boyfriend?" Maya asked. "Brent Miles? Do you know anything about him? Had he argued with Christine at all? Was there any reason that he might have wanted to hurt her?"

Statistically, when it came to the murders of women, partners and spouses were far and away the most common culprits. It made sense to at least look into that direction.

"I think the police looked at him," Jason Weller said. "But they concluded that he had an alibi. In any case, I can't imagine him wanting to hurt our daughter."

Maya had already heard the alibi from Reyes. In the face of it, and with no additional motive, it was hard to justify looking further at the boyfriend.

"Can you tell us more about Christine's life?" Maya asked, wanting to change tack. The police would have asked these questions at the time of her murder. "What did she do outside of work? What were her hobbies?"

"She liked to read," Sinead said. "She would go out to art galleries."

"Was she popular?" Maya asked. "Lots of friends?"

She saw Dina nod. "I have their details if you want them."

"Thank you," Maya said. "Was there *anyone* else you can think of who might have wanted to hurt Christine?"

Both of her parents were already shaking their heads. It was Christine's father who answered.

"No, I'm sorry. Just the idea of anyone disliking our daughter that much is hard to comprehend."

"I understand," Maya said. She took out a card and set it down on the arm of the armchair. "If you think of anything else, anything at all, please call me."

"I'll show you out," Dina said. She led the way to the door, going outside with Maya and Marco. There was a slightly troubled look on her face as she did it.

"What is it, Dina?" Maya asked. "Was there something that you couldn't say in front of your parents?"

"It might be nothing," Dina said.

"Tell me anyway," Maya suggested. "Whatever it is, I'll listen."

"It's just… something has always seemed a bit off about Brent's alibi for that night. I know Christine loved him, but I never trusted him. I tried telling the police at the time, but they ignored it. I think you should take a closer look at him."

Maya nodded. "Thank you, Dina. I might just do that."

CHAPTER NINE

Maya sat outside Brent Miles's home, taking the time to look him up on the FBI's systems before she and Marco went in to speak with him.

The house was tucked away at the end of a lane, backing onto a stretch of parkland. It probably made for a beautiful place to live, but Maya found herself thinking about it more in terms of how easy it would be for someone to slip out of the house if they wanted to avoid talking to the FBI. If Brent was caught up in all of this, Maya would have to be ready for him to run.

As she read the police files on him, she found her interest in Christine Weller's former boyfriend starting to grow.

"A few DUIs," Maya said. "A couple of arrests for bar fights. Onc for hitting a former girlfriend."

"So he has a violent streak," Marco said. "Including towards women. This has to have come up in the original investigation, though."

"I guess, once they heard that he had an alibi, none of that mattered anymore," Maya replied.

"But Christine's sister thinks otherwise." Marco looked intrigued. "Is that just her disliking him, or does she know something we don't?"

"That's the question," Maya said.

It was possible that Dina simply had a problem with her sister's former boyfriend, so that when Christine died, her suspicions automatically went his way. Maya had the impression that there was more to it than that, though. At the very least, they needed to check this. If there was some kind of flaw with Brent Miles's alibi, then maybe they could find their murderer quickly.

She and Marco approached the door, and Maya knocked. In spite of her misgivings when it came to Brent's file, she reminded herself that this was just an interview to gain more information, at least for now. She had nothing to make her treat him as a suspect beyond one vague comment from Christine's sister.

The man who opened the door was in his thirties, a little taller than Maya, and looked as though he'd just woken up. At least, he was wrapped up in a robe, and was rubbing his eyes. He was obviously in shape, and good looking in a square jawed, athletic kind of way. Of course, it was hard to think of a man as attractive when she'd just seen on his record what he could be like with women.

"What is it?" he asked.

"Brent Miles? I'm Agent Grey, with the FBI. This is Detective Spinelli. We're reinvestigating the death of Christine Weller, and since you were her boyfriend at the time, we were hoping that you might be able to tell us more about her."

It seemed best to keep it neutral for now, find out what Brent knew before she started asking about his alibi.

Maya caught the nervous flick of his eyes back towards the house. He obviously wasn't entirely happy about her and Marco showing up at his door.

"I guess you'd better come in. Ellie, we have company. The FBI."

He led the way through to a kitchen space where Maya seated herself at a breakfast bar.

"Coffee?" Brent asked.

"Please," Maya said.

A woman came in as Brent was making the coffee, also wrapped up in a robe, and now Maya started to get the impression that there hadn't been a lot of sleeping going on after all. The woman was probably in her mid-twenties, with jet black hair, mid-brown skin and dark eyes. She smiled over at Maya as she came into the kitchen, but to Maya, the smile didn't quite seem to reach her eyes. Instead, she looked slightly worried.

Maya didn't read anything into that just yet. It was normal for people to be worried when the FBI came calling.

Then again, it might also have something to do with the part where Brent seemed to have moved on pretty quickly from his last girlfriend's death. He'd found someone else so quickly? When everyone else around Christine was wrapped up in their grief? It didn't necessarily mean anything, because people all dealt with death in their own ways, but it did surprise Maya a little.

Brent passed Maya and Marco coffee, and Maya sipped hers before starting with her first question.

"Can you tell me about Christine?"

“She was a wonderful person,” Brent said. “It wasn’t just that she was a teacher, she was always helping out with something, trying to do some good in the community.”

“What kinds of things?” Maya asked.

It took Brent several seconds to think of something. Maya found herself wondering if that meant that there weren’t quite as many good deeds as he’d suggested or if he hadn’t really been paying attention to Christine’s life.

“Well, she organized some yard sales for local charities. She helped out with some after school clubs, that kind of thing.”

Maya made a mental note of that. The odds were that the killer had met her somewhere in the course of her normal life, so the more Maya knew about that life, the better.

“Do you know who her friends were?” Maya asked.

“I met some of them,” Brent said. “I mostly only knew first names, though. We didn’t keep in touch after her death. You’d probably be better off talking to that sister of hers for that kind of thing.”

Maya caught the sharpness of his tone as he said that. “You didn’t get along with Dina?”

She could see Marco watching him as intently as she was. If there was some kind of tension there, then they needed to know about it.

“It’s not that we didn’t get along, exactly,” Brent said.

“You’re sure?” Marco said. “She doesn’t seem to like you much.”

It was a blunt way to put it, but Maya guessed that he’d decided it was exactly what Brent needed. He had to be called out on the little lies so that he would know that he couldn’t get away with any bigger ones. And because he’d been the one to do it, Maya could continue playing good cop for now. Ellie stood in the corner, apparently not knowing whether to contribute anything or not.

“Ok, ok, we didn’t get along,” Brent said. “She always thought that I wasn’t good enough for her sister. She thought I was some kind of screw up, and Christine was perfect.”

There was enough bitterness there to make Maya ask the next question. “She *wasn’t* perfect, then?”

“She was… well, maybe she tried too hard to be perfect, and she wanted everyone around her to be too.”

Maya glanced across to Marco, and he took his cue to play bad cop again. “Everyone, or just you? Did the two of you argue?”

Brent was already shaking his head before Marco had finished asking the question.

"I don't know what you heard, but it's all lies."

That was too quick, and too much of a protestation for Maya.

"We hadn't heard anything, Brent. What lies are we meant to have heard?"

Brent shook his head. "I don't know. People talk. They make it sound as though everything was wrong between us. The cops looked at me like I was this obvious suspect."

Maya decided that she couldn't let that go, either. "They looked at you because you have multiple arrests for violence, Brent. Those bar fights, what was it? Someone looked at your girlfriend the wrong way? Someone tried to muscle in on what was yours?"

"It wasn't like that," Brent said. "They were just fights. Fights happen sometimes, even somewhere like here. Everyone wants to pretend that this is a perfect little town, where nothing more exciting than a few boardgames ever happens, but it's not."

"What about the other arrest, Brent?" Maya asked. "The one where you slapped your girlfriend in the middle of a bar?"

She glanced over at Ellie as she said that, trying to gauge his new girlfriend's reaction. Did she know about this side of him?

Maya had given up on just questioning him like a witness. It was obvious that he didn't know enough about Christine's life to help that way, but he was holding back enough that Maya was starting to believe in him as a suspect.

"That was a mistake, and one I've regretted ever since. But that wasn't Christine."

As if that made it all better. As if there was no chance that he would ever hurt *her*. Strangely, Ellie seemed to be okay with it. She really had heard it before. Or she just loved him that much.

Maya could see the fear building on his face.

"Tell me," Maya said. "How long have you been seeing… Ellie, isn't it?"

"A little while," Brent said. Maya could hear the defensiveness there, trying to push back against the question.

"It looks as though you moved on pretty quickly, Brent."

"I know what you're thinking. What Christine's family thinks. What the police thought. That I'm just some scumbag who obviously just wants to hurt women. That I must have killed her. Well, it wasn't me. I had an alibi."

He dropped that into the conversation as if it should stop everything dead. Instead, Maya kept going.

"What was your alibi again, Brent?"

She wanted to hear him say it, wanted to hear the details directly from him.

"I was out drinking with the guys. We went to a few bars, and then to a few more, until we couldn't even remember where we were. We stayed out the whole night, until sunrise, and then I ended up walking back home. By the time I got there, there were already something like a dozen messages waiting for me, wanting to tell me what had happened."

It was an impressive story, one that put him in the company of plenty of witnesses, and made it clear that he couldn't possibly have been the killer. There was only one problem with it:

Maya was sure that he was lying.

"That's not the alibi you gave to the police at the time," Maya pointed out.

"Yes it is," Brent said.

"Nearly, but not quite. When you talked to the police, you told them that you went out drinking, then crashed on a friend's floor. You even showed them photos of your night out."

"That's nothing," Brent said. "So I got the detail wrong, so what?"

Marco stepped in, obviously getting it.

"You don't remember exactly what you were doing the night your girlfriend was killed?" Marco asked. "You don't remember every detail of that night perfectly?"

Maya didn't believe it either, which begged the question of what Brent was trying to hide.

"Why are you lying to us, Brent?" Maya asked.

"I'm not lying." He couldn't look at her while he said it, though.

"You're hiding something," Maya said. "It's better if you just come out and tell us what it is."

"I didn't kill Christine." He was looking more uncomfortable by the second. Maya had the feeling that with just a couple more questions, she would be able to get him to tell her the truth.

"Then where were you that night?" Maya asked. "I believe that you went drinking, but I'm sure that when I ask all of your friends, they won't actually remember where you were after that. Where were you? What were you doing?"

"He was with me!" Ellie blurted it out from the side. "He was with me, ok?"

Maya paused, taking that new information in. It sounded like the truth, but even so, it took her several seconds to process it.

"Is that true, Brent?" Maya asked. "Were you with Ellie, here?"

Brent looked as uncomfortable as if Maya had told him that she was convinced he'd killed Christine.

"Yes," he said, looking across to Ellie, not to Maya, as he did it. "Things with Christine weren't great, and Ellie and I had gotten close."

"You were seeing her behind your girlfriend's back," Marco said. Maya could hear the disapproval there.

"Do you think I don't know that we did things the wrong way?" Brent snapped back. "That I should have just been honest? But Ellie and I, we're in love in a way that I don't think I ever really was with Christine. I tried to hold back, but…"

"But you got drunk that night, and went over to see her anyway," Maya finished for him. She saw him nod. "And then you lied to the police."

Brent gave a sheepish nod. "I knew how bad it would look. They'd assume that I killed Christine so that I could be with Ellie, or that I tried to break up with her and things went bad."

Maya briefly considered those possibilities. The problem in both cases was that his new girlfriend swore that he'd been with her that night. It didn't leave enough time for him to be the killer. Was it possible that she was lying to protect him?

"Do you have any proof?" Maya asked.

Ellie was there then, holding out her phone. There was a picture on it, of her and Brent together, out in front of one of the game piece statues that counted as landmarks in Hastel. There was a time stamp on the photograph.

They had proof. They'd been together that night.

The only way this wouldn't be real was if they'd planned the whole thing carefully together. Maya didn't buy that, though. The crime that night had been something planned well in advance. Even after such a short conversation, Maya didn't think that Brent was the kind of person who could plan something like that. Maybe he could lash out at strangers when he was drunk, but cold-blooded murder was a different matter.

It meant that Maya needed a new suspect. She was going to have to go back to the case files and start over.

Maya and Marco left the house. She was surprised to find that it was already getting dark. The journey there, and then the initial investigations, had taken longer than she thought.

"We should get back to the precinct and look at the files," Maya said.

Marco was already shaking his head. "In the morning, Maya."

Maya wanted to argue, wanted to tell him that she would keep going without him if she had to. Marco, of all people, knew what was on the line here.

"You have to pace yourself, Maya," Marco insisted. "Pick this up in the morning."

Maya gave in. "All right, but first thing tomorrow, we go into the precinct and start over with this."

CHAPTER TEN

Frank had kept eyes on Tori Blauer for a while now, through intermediaries and through electronic surveillance, but it was very different seeing her up close for the first time.

She was slender and tanned, dark haired and, Frank supposed, very pretty, not that such things truly touched him. If it had just been pretty girls that he needed for what he was trying to do, well, the world was full of them. He wouldn't have had to go to the lengths that he did, both in collecting his bunnies and in his… other work.

There were far fewer women out there who fit his real requirements, so that it took far more effort to actually find them. Tori was one of them.

Currently, Frank was sitting on the outside of a small café, watching Tori as she moved around a shopping precinct. Frank watched her go into an art supplies store, and he didn't need to follow her in there to know what she would buy. He already had a copy of the shopping list that she'd written on her phone: cerulean blue paint, a triple 0 brush, some paint thinner.

Not that she would have a chance to use them.

For the moment, Frank kept his position. He wasn't worried about cameras spotting him there. He was just one more person among the many out there, while his hat and dark glasses meant that it was going to be hard for anyone to pick him out later. For the moment, he was just a man enjoying his coffee, people watching while the world went by. He made small jottings in a notebook as he sat there, so that anyone watching would think that he was some kind of writer looking for inspiration.

Frank already had his inspiration. He had his purpose, and Tori was going to be a part of it. She was going to help to make his great work complete.

She didn't know that yet, of course. She would be thinking about her graduation from the MFA she'd just completed, about the show that would show off her work and provide her introduction to the art world.

Frank kept watching her as she went around to the other stores there. As she got further away, he stood, following from a safe distance.

He'd had one of his little helpers do all of this up to this point. After all, Tori had been a contingency plan, not the main focus of his efforts. Now though… he didn't want to leave this part of things to others. When it came to snatching her off the street, Frank was sure that he could have others do it perfectly competently, but he wasn't about to take the chance. Some things were better to take care of personally.

Tori set off out of the shopping precinct, walking as usual, taking the same route home that she had every time she'd visited. Frank knew that, was banking on that fact. He'd already picked out the spot along that route where he would strike.

Carefully, he kept pace with her, not wanting to get too close, but wanting to make it easy for him to close the distance between them when the time came. He wove among the pedestrians, trying not to stand out too much. Being unseen was the most crucial part of all of this.

The crowds were thinning out now, as Frank had known they would. Now, it was just him and his target moving along the street, towards the spot where another alley opened onto it.

Towards the spot where he'd parked a van, ready and waiting.

Frank took out a syringe. For his other work, he didn't bother with such aids; he didn't need them. For this, though… he'd found that a sedative helped his bunnies to transition to their new lives smoothly, without the risk of hurting them unnecessarily as he took them.

Frank started to move closer, advancing on his prey. In just a few strides, he would be up close to her. Then there would be no preamble, no talking, no chance for her to see him. He would put the sedative into her, grab her, and get her off the street as quickly as possible. He would leave no opening for this to go wrong.

She would probably try to fight back. She'd taken a self-defense course once, although it didn't seem to be helping now, since Tori hadn't even glanced around at him in the time he'd been following her. It wouldn't make any difference anyway. A couple of hours' training couldn't do anything against the kind of training he'd had.

A few more steps. He'd planned this moment. Everything was set up for him to strike.

Then he saw the young man coming down the street in the other direction. He threw out his arms and Tori went to him, hugging him tightly. From his observations of her, Frank recognized one of her friends. A friend who shouldn't have been there.

"Tori! Greta told me that you'd gone to the art store, so I thought I'd come catch up to you. You want to go get coffee?"

"Sounds good," Tori said.

It sounded awful to Frank. If she'd said that she didn't have any time, then there might still have been a chance to take her now, the moment her friend moved away.

Frank forced himself to walk past, not even hesitating.

There was no opportunity.

That wasn't strictly true. It would be the easiest thing in the world to simply deal with the young man. Frank had weapons on him. He could step in close, use the sedative on Tori, kill the young man with a knife, and be gone from there before anyone could come to help.

Frank didn't want to do that, though. A part of it was caution. He didn't take risks that he didn't need to. Why take the risk that Tori might get away in the moments it took to kill her friend?

The other part of it was simple: it didn't fit with any of the rules that kept order through all of this. It wasn't a full moon, and the young man hadn't broken any of the rules of Frank's game. Yes, he *could* kill him, but it was better to just keep moving.

So Frank walked past the two of them, heading into the alley and getting into his van. He walked within a couple of feet of them to do it, and neither of them even noticed. This wasn't the right moment, but his chance would come.

He would have his new bunny soon enough, and next time, he would strike in a spot where he could control the whole environment.

CHAPTER ELEVEN

They started fresh the next morning, and Maya found it frustrating that they had to. She'd been hoping that their first day on the case would at least start to point them in the right direction. Instead of a murderer, though, all they'd found was that Christine Weller's boyfriend had been seeing someone else.

It had gotten them precisely nowhere.

"What are we working on today?" Marco asked as they headed into Hastel's police department, taking the stairs up to the second floor.

"I want to go through the files," Maya said. "I had Reyes skim them for me before, but that doesn't give me everything. I want to go through the originals in detail. There might be something there that isn't in the versions they sent over."

"You want me to help you read through?" Marco asked.

Maya shook her head. She wanted to do that part herself. It only worked if she had all the information in her head, ready to pull the strands together.

"I want you to start contacting Christine's friends. My guess is that contact details for at least some of them will be in the file. If not, you can get them from Christine's sister."

"And when she asks how things went with Brent?"

That was a good question, because it was hard to imagine that Dina wouldn't ask, so soon after pointing the two of them at her sister's former boyfriend.

"Just tell her that we're satisfied that he isn't the one who killed Christine."

"Are we?" Marco asked. "There's still a possibility that his new girlfriend could be providing him with an alibi to cover up the death of the old one."

Maya had to admit that it was possible. People had done far worse for the ones they loved. Even so, she didn't think it was likely.

"The photograph they showed us suggests otherwise. I think they were telling the truth," she said. "And why kill Christine? Why not just break up with her, if Brent didn't want to be with her? It all rests on the idea that he would see murdering her as the only possible way to end their relationship."

If they'd been married, then maybe it might have made for more of a motive. There had been plenty of people who had killed their spouses rather than risking losing everything in a divorce, but for someone Brent wasn't even living with, it made no sense.

"I guess so," Marco said. "Although it means we have to start over."

"Then we start over," Maya said. "As many times as we need to."

So long as they did it quickly. A week wasn't a long time to solve a case, especially now that they'd used up their first day.

"It's easy to forget just how determined you can be sometimes," Marco said. He sounded impressed, although Maya also knew how worried he'd been in previous cases that she might be getting obsessed. Maya wished that she could promise him that it wouldn't come to that here, but the truth was that she would do whatever it took to keep solving cases and see women released.

They reached the second floor and Maya looked around until she spotted Detective Simms. He came over as soon as he saw them, and Maya found herself wondering if that was eagerness to help with the case, or determination that they wouldn't interfere with the smooth running of the department.

"We've found an office for you both. It's just over here."

He led the way to what was probably normally used as a conference room. It was large, open and empty. For once, Maya didn't seem to have been tucked away from the rest of the department.

"If you need anything," Detective Simms said, "let me know."

"Is the case file you gave me the original copy?" Maya asked.

"Looking to see what we put in our notes?"

Maya decided to be honest. "Yes. I need the facts of the case, but I also want to understand what the thinking was."

Maya knew from experience that what cops thought among themselves and what went into the case files were often two different things.

"I can *tell* you that," Detective Simms said. "We didn't have anything to go on. We tried looking at the boyfriend, but he had an alibi. Beyond that, Christine Weller didn't have anyone who might have wanted to kill her. If it's really not the Moonlight Killer…"

"It isn't."

“Then I don’t know who it could be.”

Maya could understand the worry in his tone. Before, his department had at least a theory when it came to Christine’s death. One that meant the people of the town weren’t in danger. The Moonlight Killer had moved on. Eventually, he might be caught, and they could call the case closed. Now, though, they all had to find new places to look.

“I’ll get you the original file,” Detective Simms promised, and hurried off to do it.

Marco got out his phone and started to call Dina, while Maya could at least look through the electronic variations of the file.

“Hi Dina, this is Detective Spinelli, from the other day. Yes, we did. No, I’m sorry, but we don’t think so. Which means we still need to keep looking. Do you have contact details for any of your sister’s friends? It will help us to look for anything else in her life that might have led someone to want to hurt her. Yes, I know, but please, you need to trust that we can do this.”

It sounded as though Marco was having a little trouble getting past Dina’s suspicions about her sister’s boyfriend, but she trusted that he would be able to do it. Marco had a kind of charm to him that was hard to resist.

Or maybe that was just with her.

For the moment, Maya forced herself to look away from Marco and focused on looking over the crime scene photographs. She saw Christine Weller lying there just a stride or two from the front door to her house, just a couple of steps from safety, with a ligature still fastened tight around her throat.

She lay face up, which, if the killer had strangled her from behind, suggested that he’d turned her over afterwards. Would that mean that he’d left forensic traces? Maya went looking through the files for a forensics report while behind her, Marco kept going with the calls.

“I was just wondering if anything had changed in Christine’s life shortly before her death?” Marco asked the friend he was currently on the phone with. “Anything at all, no matter how small. Did she seem worried about anything? No, I understand it’s hard to go back over it all, but anything you remember might help.”

Maya started to go through the forensics report. It was pretty sparse. The killer had left the ligature he’d used around Christine Weller’s throat, but there had been no traces of DNA on it. That suggested someone careful, someone who knew what they were doing when it came to killing. Murders were rarely so neat, but the killer had been exacting in their execution of this one.

Maya went back to the crime scene photographs. There were no obvious defensive wounds on Christine Weller, no sign that she'd even had a chance to fight back. She'd been taken by surprise, and killed quickly.

If it weren't for the timing, and the fact of who had sent her to look at this case, even Maya *might* have believed that it was the work of the Moonlight Killer. There was a precision to it that reminded her of his work, and the method of the killing was definitely consistent.

Detective Simms chose that moment to walk back into their makeshift office, bringing a fat version of the file with him. He set it down in front of Maya.

"Here you go. Although I don't know if there will be anything in there that we didn't already work through."

"I want to make sure," Maya said, while in the background, Marco was still making calls.

"I know it's strange me calling like this, but can you think of anyone, anyone at all, who might have a reason to hurt Christine?"

It was the kind of work that would ordinarily have taken a whole team a week or more, but Maya and Marco had to compress it into a few days if they were still going to have enough time to catch the killer at the end of all this.

It meant that Maya had to go through the original report, page by page, trying to find something that might point them in the right direction. She started by trying to find the places where the file Detective Simms had given them differed from the copy she'd seen.

She went to the same crime scene photographs that she'd just been looking at, trying to find anything that didn't fit. Maya spotted something there almost immediately, a note clipped to the page, written in spidery handwriting that was close to illegible. It was the kind of thing that didn't make it into electronic copies, which meant that it was exactly the kind of thing she was looking for.

Maya did her best with it, treating it like any other piece of evidence that needed to be slowly picked apart. She found that, by squinting slightly, she could start to make out the individual letters.

Contents of victim's bag

Maya realized that she could see a bag lying in the picture, almost out of shot. It must have fallen there when she'd been struggling, trying to get the rope from around her neck. The list told Maya what she'd been carrying at the time, and even if she didn't think it would give her many clues, Maya started to pick her way through it, making sure.

Most of it was the kind of stuff anyone might have kept in a purse, the kinds of things that Maya stuffed into her own when she carried one. A pair of spectacles, some money, a small notebook, a phone.

One slightly strange word stood at the end of the list, and it took Maya several more seconds to work out the letters of it.

Puzzle.

Maya put her head out of the door to their office and found Detective Simms there by a water cooler.

He came back into the office.

"Detective Simms," Maya asked the detective, "do you have any idea what this is?"

"Puzzle?" Detective Simms said. Maya saw him pinch the bridge of his nose, obviously trying to think. "Oh, I remember. There was a jigsaw piece in her purse."

"A jigsaw piece?"

The detective had said it as if it were something perfectly normal, but to Maya, it seemed utterly odd and out of place.

"People have all kinds of strange things in their pockets and purses," Detective Simms said. "Especially here in Hastel."

He made it sound as if it didn't matter, yet instinct made Maya latch onto it as something out of place, something that shouldn't have been there. There was no reason for a teacher to have a single piece from a jigsaw puzzle sitting randomly in her purse.

"Marco, what do you think about the victim having a puzzle piece in her purse when she was killed?" Maya asked.

"It sounds odd to me," Marco replied.

"You both think a *puzzle piece* is important?" Detective Simms said. "Here?"

Maya nodded. The town might call itself the boardgame capital of America, but that still didn't make the presence of the piece any more normal. It sounded less like something that the victim might have put there herself… and more like the kind of thing a killer might have left.

"Is the puzzle piece still here?" Maya asked.

She saw Detective Simms shrug.

“It should still be down in evidence.”

“Can we check?” Maya asked.

The detective shrugged again, but led the way out of the office with Maya and Marco following. The three of them walked down a couple of flights of stairs, down to the basement level of the police department. They followed Detective Simms through a couple of doors, to a big evidence lock up, where a bulky sergeant sat at a counter, watching over everything there.

“Hey Jim,” Detective Simms said. “I need something from the Weller case. Can you get out the contents of her purse?”

“Sure, no problem. Wait here a minute.”

The sergeant disappeared through a door, leaving Maya tapping her feet in impatience. Every time she had to wait, it was impossible not to think of her sister, stuck somewhere in the Moonlight Killer’s power.

The sergeant came back with an evidence box, opening it up for the three of them to look through. It didn’t take long for Maya to spot the jigsaw piece, and she fished it out of the box, holding it up to look at the pattern. It was big, almost the size of her hand.

It was hard to see what was on the piece, because it was only a tiny fragment of some larger design. Most of it seemed to be taken up with a wood pattern, as if from a tree in some kind of landscape.

Maya didn’t know if it meant anything or not, but somehow, she felt that it had some significance. Now, she just had to find out what it meant.

CHAPTER TWELVE

Where was Maya meant to start to look for connections to puzzle pieces? In a town like Hastel, the answer to that seemed to her to be "everywhere." The whole place was filled with boardgame connections, but Maya needed something more specific if she was going to make progress.

"Why would the jigsaw piece be there?" Marco asked as the two of them headed back up to the office.

"Why not, in this town?" Detective Simms countered. "You're making too much of this. You think I can't walk across my kitchen floor at night without stepping on three game pieces my kids have left out?"

"This wasn't a floor, though," Maya pointed out. "It wasn't some random litter. It was her bag. Tell me, Detective, if I asked you to turn out your pockets right now, would there be a puzzle piece there?"

"Well, no," the detective admitted.

Maya doubted that it would be the case for anyone there in the station, in spite of the town's boardgame obsession. She hurried up to the second floor, leading the way back towards their office.

"So, if it's not a usual thing to have, why was it there?"

"I still think it's just coincidence," Detective Simms said. He held up his hands. "But this is your case. I should be getting on with my own work. You want to chase after puzzle pieces, that's your business."

In other words, he didn't want to be associated with whatever craziness the FBI was trying. That was fine by Maya. He'd given them enough help to at least get started, and Maya had a much better sounding board than the detective.

"Why was it there, Marco?"

"You think it was placed there deliberately?" Marco looked as if he understood. Maybe it was just the time that they'd spent working together. After all, by this point, Marco probably knew Maya about as well as anyone.

"It *might* be a coincidence," Maya said. She'd seen enough as an agent to know that sometimes, things were just random. Trying to ascribe meaning to them could be dangerous. “But what if it isn’t? What if someone put it there? Why do something like that?”

“Because it means something to them,” Marco said. “Or as a calling card. Are you saying that this is a serial killer?”

Was Maya saying that? Serial killers often took trophies or left calling cards, and something like this could potentially be exactly that. It could be a killer actively looking to grab attention, trying to get themselves labelled as the “jigsaw killer” in the press.

“I don’t know yet,” Maya said. “Maybe, but we only have the one killing to go by. At the very least, though, you’re right, and this means something to the killer. If we can work out what, then it gives us a better chance of finding them.”

“So how do we use all of this?” Marco said.

That was the question. It was one thing having a hunch about a possibility. It was quite another finding the evidence they needed to back it up.

“If this *is* some kind of serial killer, then the first thing to look for is whether this motif has been repeated anywhere else,” Maya said. “We go through police files and try to find any references to puzzle pieces.”

“You check the computers,” Marco suggested. “I’ll check with Detective Simms to see if he’s heard about any other cases.”

Maya nodded. It made sense for them to make as much use of local resources as they could while they were doing this. Especially when the initial mention of the puzzle piece hadn’t been there in the main file.

Maya went to her laptop and logged into the FBI’s systems. She had access to police databases through there, so she could start to formulate some searches to scour the files.

She started by searching for the words “puzzle” and “jigsaw” in police files from Hastel. There were a few hits for the first word, which meant that Maya had to go into each report, trying to find them in their context.

What she found wasn’t promising. The reports talked about a witness being puzzled, or about some puzzling aspect of the case, not about a physical puzzle piece. As far as Maya could make out, there hadn’t been any similar cases in the town.

She broadened her search, widening it to include surrounding towns and cities. The only problem with doing that to get more hits was that Maya got *far* more hits, the amount of information almost overwhelming. It meant dozens of reports stacking up on Maya's screen, so that it was slow going, working through them all.

Maya pinched the bridge of her nose. This was what her job usually came down to, when she wasn't rushing trying to keep up with the Moonlight Killer's whims. Grinding her way through the evidence, trying to find any hint of something that told her the truth of what was going on.

As she worked her way through the files, it became clear that these weren't any more relevant than the ones from Hastel. Again, the word "puzzle" was coming up in ordinary usage, not because someone had found a piece of a jigsaw puzzle sitting in another bag.

Marco came back and Maya looked up at him hopefully.

"Anything?"

"Simms says that he hasn't seen another case with a puzzle piece. He hasn't heard of one, either."

So there was nothing in the files, and the local cops hadn't heard of anything similar. Was it possible that it really *was* all just a coincidence? Was Maya wasting precious time by chasing after a clue that didn't mean anything? That was the danger with a tempting piece of evidence like this: it was possible to spend too much time on it, and not look at something simpler.

"Marco, am I doing the wrong thing, looking at this?" Maya asked. "Should I be looking at something else?"

Marco looked worried then.

"What is it?" Maya asked.

"I'm just not used to hearing you doubt yourself," Marco said.

Maya smiled slightly at that. "Normally it's the opposite, I think. You having to hold me back before I run off and do something I shouldn't."

Marco had the sense not to answer that directly, it seemed. "I trust you, Maya. If you think this jigsaw piece is important, then it's important. We need to find another way of finding a connection."

The only question was who else they could talk to about it. If even the cops didn't remember anything to do with puzzle pieces, who else would have spent enough time around the victims of murders to potentially spot such a thing?

The answer came to Maya almost immediately.

"We need to talk to the coroner."

*

To Maya, the waiting area of the morgue looked far too much like a doctor's waiting room, decorated with cheerful prints depicting the boards for a bewildering variety of different games, which seemed to add an element of whimsy to the place that felt a little at odds with its serious purpose. It had a few chairs and a reception desk, and even old magazines set out on a table.

The man who stepped out to meet them had to be sixty, with white hair, a close-trimmed beard, and a portly body. He was wearing a plastic apron and gloves over a suit.

"Hello, can I help you?"

"I'm Agent Grey, with the FBI," Maya said. "This is Detective Spinelli, who is consulting with me."

It still seemed so strange to introduce Marco like that, but what else could Maya say he was?

"I'm Dr. Chalkins," the coroner said. "Forgive me if I don't shake hands, but you caught me in the middle of an autopsy. A traffic death, so quite messy."

It made Maya glad that they were standing in the middle of a pleasant waiting room, rather than in the main room of the place, watching a body being cut open, measured, assessed.

She found herself having a flashback to the sight of the finger that had come to her in a box. Maya felt bile rise in her throat, but held herself together while she forced herself to smile at the coroner.

"You're here investigating the Christine Weller murder?" Dr. Chalkins asked.

Maya nodded. "How did you know?"

"Oh, you're big news around town. It's not every day we get an FBI agent here. Are you here to talk about my findings from that autopsy? I'm afraid it was all rather straightforward. Simple strangulation with the ligature found with the body. No defensive wounds, and no additional forensic evidence."

"And nothing that wasn't in your report?" Marco asked. "No suspicions that didn't make it there?"

"Nothing, I'm sorry," Dr. Chalkins said. "If I'd had such suspicions, I would have included a side note in the file."

Maya had expected that might be the case, although she was glad that Marco had at least asked the question. It was good to know for sure that there wasn't anything else that hadn't made it into the file that might come around to ambush them later.

All that was left was for her to bring up the reason she'd come here. Maya took out the piece that she'd gotten out of evidence, with its image of a log.

"Do you remember this?" Maya said.

"I don't believe I've seen it before," Dr. Chalkins said.

"It was found among Christine Weller's effects," Maya explained. "I think it might be significant. Have you seen any other deaths where puzzle pieces have been found?"

She wasn't hopeful, because if the coroner hadn't seen the things that had been found with Christine Weller's body, then there was no reason to believe that he would see them from other cases.

Yet she saw the moment when a thoughtful look came over Dr. Chalkins's face.

"That *does* spark some kind of memory," he said. "What was it? Where have I… oh, yes, of course."

He beckoned for them to follow him through into the autopsy room. Maya forced herself to follow, doing everything she could to ignore the sight of a body laid out on a steel gurney as she kept pace with the coroner. The scent of death and preserving fluids made her want to throw up, but she ignored the urge. He led the way through it and out the far side, into an office space. There were several rows of large filing cabinets along one wall.

"Normally, the police hold onto evidence," Dr. Chalkins said. "But when we find things in an autopsy that aren't taken as evidence, we hold onto them until family members claim them. There was a case… I don't know, perhaps ten months ago? Give me a moment."

He opened one of the file drawers, searching through it. He came out with both a file and with something else, something that caught Maya's eye: a single puzzle piece, held between his thumb and forefinger.

"I found this during the autopsy of a young woman called Trinity Dee. It was tucked into her left sock, where no one would initially find it."

And definitely in a spot where it wouldn't have gotten by accident. Someone had put it there deliberately. Either Trinity… or her killer.

"I mentioned it to the detectives at the time, but they didn't feel that it was significant," Dr. Chalkins said.

They didn't think it was significant? Maya could barely believe that. Surely, they should have followed up on something like this?

"They told you that this is Hastel, and puzzle pieces get everywhere?" Marco asked.

The coroner nodded. "I see you've heard that before."

Maya took the file, starting to look through it, barely able to believe that the detectives on the case hadn't made anything of the piece. Was that just a small-town thing? Did they see so little serious crime here that they'd forgotten what they were meant to do when one occurred?

Maya kept reading, hoping to find an answer. The first thing that struck her was the photograph of the victim. She was perhaps thirty, dark haired and slender. At first glance, she looked almost identical to Christine Weller, so that it was only by looking closer that Maya started to see the differences between their features. Trinity had a slightly more upturned nose, slightly broader cheeks.

Even so, the similarities were remarkable. They could have been sisters.

"How was Trinity Dee killed?" Maya asked.

"Strangulation, with a ligature."

The same method. Maya held out her hand for the puzzle piece, and started to turn it over and over in her hand, studying it. It was the same size as the one that had been found with Christine Weller, perhaps even from the same puzzle, but this one showed a section of what appeared to be a stream.

Were the two a part of some nature puzzle? Maya took out the first puzzle piece, but it didn't seem to connect naturally to the second. She couldn't even be certain that the two were from the same puzzle; that much was just a hunch.

One thing was certain though, because there were too many connections to deny it:

They were dealing with a serial killer. One who was clearly into puzzles.

They needed to find out more about puzzles, and fast.

CHAPTER THIRTEEN

Maya needed to know about puzzles, and it seemed as though she and Marco might be in the right town to find out everything there was to know. Hastel had far more games stores than anywhere its size seemed to have a right to, so that Maya was almost spoiled for choice when trying to find one.

She settled on the store closest to the police department, which turned out to be a broad storefront, so filled up with comics, boardgame covers, and posters for D&D expansions that it was hard to see inside.

When Maya actually stepped inside, she found herself in a brightly lit space that seemed to be half-filled with displays for various products, and half-filled with tables around which people were sitting, playing a variety of games. Some were sitting around boards, moving pieces, others holding brightly printed cards, laying them down one by one. A few were playing role playing games, rolling dice and making notes on character sheets.

Maya had been expecting kids, and there were a few teenagers in there, but there were more adults: mainly men with a few women. Maya took a moment or two to look around the store displays until she finally found a selection of jigsaw puzzles tucked away behind everything else, almost as if the place were embarrassed about them.

"Can I help you?" a woman in her twenties asked. She was wearing jeans, a t-shirt with *The DM's word is FINAL* in big letters, and a long coat that looked more like it should be in some historical re-enactment group than for daily wear. Maya made out a name badge that said "Clary."

"Are you looking for something specific?" she asked. "Or maybe you'd like to join a game?"

Maya took out her ID.

"I need to know a little more about jigsaw puzzles," she said. "It's in connection with a case."

"Jigsaw puzzles?" Clary shrugged. "We have a few. Some people do them because they find it soothing, or whatever."

Clearly, she wasn't one of those people. Judging by how few there were in the store, it wasn't the place's main focus.

"You're not a fan of them?" Marco asked.

"I just think they're really… you know, solitary. Like, why spend hours doing one of those when you could spend the same hours playing a game with half a dozen friends? I know there's all the bullshit about how William Hastel founded this town on jigsaw puzzles, but they do more real games these days."

"Founded the town on jigsaw puzzles?" Maya said.

Clary looked a little surprised, as if it were something that everyone who came to Hastel knew automatically, but quickly recovered. "Oh, yeah, I guess you wouldn't have heard it. Basically, Old Man Hastel, back in the 1920s or something, started paying local artists for their work and making jigsaw puzzles. Something about them caught on, and he attracted this whole local community. Now the town's named after him, there's the big factory just outside town, and… well…" She gestured to the rest of the room.

"So if I wanted to identify some jigsaw pieces, would there be a way to do that?" Maya asked.

That got a shrug from Clary. "Maybe. I couldn't do it, but if it's one of the lines they've produced up at the factory, they might know it."

Maya looked over at Marco. It seemed that they needed to pay a visit to the Hastel factory.

*

The Hastel factory was a series of buildings just outside the main town, surrounded by red brick walls that looked to Maya as though they could have been there since William Hastel had printed his first puzzle.

There was a big store set at the front, but it also had a sign above it proclaiming it to be the reception area for the rest of the building. As Maya walked in, she saw it was filled with neat rows of games, but didn't have the tables or the community atmosphere that she'd seen in the smaller store. This was boardgames as big business, not as a quiet pastime.

A young man in a red shirt emblazoned with the company logo of a die atop a jigsaw piece stood behind a counter, serving as a combination of store clerk and receptionist. It meant that Maya and

Marco had to wait in line while he served a couple of customers before she could stand in front of him and show him her ID.

"I need to speak to someone about puzzles," Maya said. "Ideally, someone who might be able to help us identify one. It's in connection with a case."

The clerk looked a little flustered. Presumably, selling boardgames wasn't often something that involved dealing with federal agents or police. He had a look that was familiar to Maya: of someone trying to catalogue every tiny illegal thing they'd ever done and trying to work out if Maya could learn about it just by looking at them.

"I… I'll see if there's anyone available to show you around."

He picked up a phone and made a call. "Hi, Tony, there are some people here from the FBI. They want some help with a case. Can you… that's great. Thanks." He hung up. "Tony will be straight through. He's one of the floor managers here. He's been here forever."

Maya took the time to look over the neat rows of board games. There were games for children, games squarely aimed at adults, and just about everything in between. Maya saw chess sets on one row, strange, cooperative games on another, but she only had eyes for the lines of jigsaw puzzles.

Maya went to them, taking out the two pieces, and trying to see if they fit with any of the puzzles that she could see. The problem with that was that she only had two puzzle pieces, when most of those on the shelf contained five hundred pieces or more. One or two claimed to have ten thousand pieces. Finding individual pieces within those might take forever.

"Hello? Are you the FBI agent?"

Maya turned to see a tall man in his sixties, with steel gray hair and a slender physique. He was wearing overalls that made him look more like a mechanic than someone who printed jigsaw puzzles for a living.

"I am," Maya said with a nod. She gestured over to Marco. "And this is Detective Spinelli."

Unlike the store clerk, this man seemed actively pleased to see them.

"I'm Tony, one of the floor managers here. Jeremy said that you need me to help you with something?"

Maya decided that the best thing was just to come out with it, so that the floor manager understood what she was trying to do. "We're looking into two murders, where puzzle pieces were found near the bodies."

"Murders?" Tony's eyes widened at that. "That's… you think it has something to do with here?"

"It's possible," Maya said. "It may be that the pieces are the killer's way of declaring some kind of connection to the factory. It's possible that he worked, or works, here."

The floor manager was already shaking his head. "Not possible. I know my guys. None of them would ever do anything like that."

That was a touching declaration of loyalty on his part, but Maya wondered if it was possible for him to really know *everyone* who worked there that well. Would he really know if there were a murderer working next to him? Even so, she decided to make it clear that wasn't the only possibility she was looking at.

"It could also be something related to the manufacturing process, or even someone who has just bought a particular puzzle because the design reflects his grand vision for the world."

"At this stage, we're keeping our options open," Marco added.

That seemed to be enough to satisfy Tony for the moment.

"Well," he said. "I guess I can begin by showing you around. Follow me."

Maya fell into step with him as he led the way out of the store. A corridor led back through into a huge factory space, dominated by long series of machines connected by conveyor belts. Maya could see plastic and metal pieces moving along those conveyor belts, falling into separate compartments, being sorted through by machines, ready to be put into boxes. Here and there, people stood, running the machines and making sure that nothing went wrong.

"We have a lot of plastic forming and metal cutting machines in here," Tony said, leading the way through it. "A few 3D printers, although for mass production, it's still easier to use molding. We save that kind of thing for the custom shop."

"The custom shop?" Maya said.

Tony gestured for her and Marco to keep following, leading the way through to a much smaller space where the machinery was on a much more human scale. There were people at desks, working with hand tools and airbrushes, as well as inputting ideas on computer screens.

"People sometimes want custom pieces made for RPGs, or even whole custom boardgames," Tony said.

"So, for gifts?" Marco asked.

"That, but also there's a thriving scene of small makers who come up with ideas for games, and then they pay us to produce small runs," Tony explained. "They hope that if they can get their game out there, it will catch attention, and blow up into something bigger."

He kept the tour going, through to a much quieter space, where a dozen different artists were working, some producing pictures, others tiny figurines.

"So, what's this?" Maya asked.

"This is our art department," Tony explained. "We still like to get in the best talent we can to paint scenes for our puzzles, but now they also produce ideas for our other games too. And obviously, in the age of digital photography, we use plenty of photographs too."

Maya watched a woman in her forties painting an idyllic hilltop scene. It wasn't the same as the one hinted at in the two pieces she'd found so far, but it at least showed her that it was possible that the puzzle might have come from here.

Maya took out the pieces, showing them to Tony.

"If these pieces came from one of your puzzles, would it be possible to tell?"

"Maybe," Tony said. He led the way over to a scanner, placing the pieces inside. "If we copy them, we can see if they fit into any of our standard patterns, then try to find the design."

"Standard patterns?" Marco asked.

For a moment or two, Maya saw surprise on Tony's face, as if it took him a second to realize that not everybody would know this kind of thing.

"Nobody cuts a fresh pattern for every puzzle. You have a number of proprietary patterns that you reuse with different pictures. There are even people out there who buy two or three puzzles with the same basic pattern and mix the pieces to create their own mash up art."

He didn't sound as if he entirely approved of that.

"So, is this one of your patterns?" Maya asked.

"Yes, I believe it may be," Tony replied. "Although it's hard to be sure with only two pieces." He pointed to a computer screen, now showing the pieces in all their detail. "Look, they're a match for H217, H3156 and H3254."

“So do the pictures match anything that you’ve produced in those patterns?” Maya asked.

It seemed that Tony was already trying to run a search to establish that. He looked up, shaking his head.

“None of our standard pictures there from our current runs. Of course, it’s possible that it might be something much older, because we don’t have all the earliest patterns digitized even now. Or it could be a custom order, some photograph someone wanted put onto a board. You can order those through us online now from anywhere.”

In a way, that was disappointing, but it was also kind of promising. A puzzle that anyone could have bought off the shelf didn’t narrow things down. One that someone might have custom ordered could still potentially lead to more, if Maya could find a way to trace it. If she could do that, then it would be as good as a fingerprint.

For now, though, she couldn’t think of a way. Instead, she had to concentrate on the other possibilities there in the factory.

“I still need a list of everyone who has worked here in the last year,” Maya said. “Just so I can narrow things down in my inquiries.”

“There’s really no point,” Tony said. “If there were a killer working here, I’d know about it.”

Maya admired the optimism of that statement. It was good to be reminded that there were still people in the world who believed that the evil among them could be spotted so easily, that a killer couldn’t walk past smiling one moment and kill someone the next.

Maya knew how different the truth was, when killers could be more or less invisible. When the Moonlight Killer was out there, and he could potentially walk right past Maya without her ever knowing that it was him.

“I still need the list,” Maya said.

She would work through it, try to find a name that led somewhere. It was her best route now to try to find the killer, and to try to do it before her time here ran out.

CHAPTER FOURTEEN

Maya was starting to regret asking for that list of employees, because it was a lot longer than she'd imagined.

"*All* these people worked here in the past year?" Maya asked, in the confines of a small office that seemed crowded with files and pieces of paper in no kind of order. If the store out front was pristine and orderly, this was the opposite, with a sense that there might be just about *anything* buried under the piles of paperwork.

She was currently holding a list that ran to three sheets, names and contact details carefully printed in rows for her to look over. There were plenty of them.

"Not all of them full time," Tony explained. "We take on a lot of casual staff when the local college breaks for summer to see if we can get any of them interested in the business. Some of them find they don't want to go back, but most do."

He made it sound more like a vocation than a normal job, the kind of thing you did and then realized that it was what you were meant to spend the rest of your life doing.

There were days when Maya felt that way about her job, but she hadn't felt that way much since a serial killer had kidnapped her sister.

"These can't all be casual staff," Maya said.

The floor manager started ticking off the rest of them on his fingers. "Then you have the artists we get in as freelancers, the consultants for things like the accounts and HR stuff, guys who take a job here because they like games, but then realize they don't like running a machine ten hours at a time… it adds up."

It certainly did. It was going to be a lot of work sorting through it all, but even with this, Maya knew that she had to ask for more information.

"Do you have HR files for these people?" she asked.

"Somewhere," Tony said. "Although I'm not sure if I should just let you go looking through people's files like that."

"This is a murder investigation," Maya reminded him, in a slightly more serious tone.

Even then, he looked doubtful. "I don't know. People won't want you looking at their files. And strictly speaking, I'm just the floor manager. I don't really have the authority."

"Then could you call someone and *get* the authority?" Maya asked.

She saw the floor manager shrug. "Mercy, she runs HR, she's on maternity leave until Thursday. Might be hard to get through to her."

Maya could feel her frustration building. Tony the floor manager had been helpful so far, but in this, he risked delaying Maya until it was too late. She couldn't afford that, not with so much at stake.

"There has to be another way," she said. "Call your boss, or something. Get permission. Remember, we're trying to catch a killer here."

The floor manager still looked troubled. "I'll tell you what I *could* do: how about we go through the names, you and me? I remember pretty much everyone who's worked here. Part of my job, really. Management don't have enough time for that kind of thing, and everyone on the factory floor is too busy doing their own work, but I meet everyone."

"And you can remember everyone on this list?" Maya asked. She had her doubts, especially when it came to letting someone who wasn't a cop or an agent this far into her investigation. But if it was the only way of getting fresh information, she was willing to try it.

"I'm pretty sure," Tony said. "And if there's anyone suspicious, *then* maybe we can have a look at their file. I'm pretty sure Mercy won't mind that."

Maya thought about it for a moment, and then nodded. It might actually save her some time, doing things this way. Besides, it meant that she got a far more human perspective of the names on the list than if she simply went through a file.

"And in the meantime, I just stand here looking pretty?" Marco said, from a corner of the office.

Maya was tempted to point out that he was good at that part, but it didn't seem like the professional thing to do, in front of a civilian. This wasn't the time to flirt with the handsome detective who kept dropping into the middle of her cases, even if she wanted to.

Did she want to? There was no denying how attracted Maya was to Marco, but she'd already shown how badly she was capable of messing things up when all her energy was going into trying to find her sister.

Maya wasn't sure that she had any time for anything else right now, however much she might want it.

Yet even now, even knowing that, at least some of her attention was on Marco most of the time, just… appreciating that he was there.

"I have an idea about that," Maya said. "Tony, you said that the puzzle pieces might be a part of one of your older designs?"

"H217 is an old pattern," the floor manager agreed. "It's possible that your pieces might fit an old puzzle using it."

"Do you have copies of any of those puzzles?"

She saw the floor manager nod, then head for the door to the office. "Wait here a minute."

He left Maya and Marco alone, waiting for him to return with whatever he'd just thought of.

"We haven't really stopped to talk since we got here," Marco said, looking over at her with an obvious note of worry. "How are you holding up?"

"It's…" Maya didn't want him looking at her with that kind of worry, like she was going to fall apart. The fact that she'd done so in front of him before now only made it worse. "I'm fine, Marco. It's good that you're here, though."

"Is it?" Marco asked. "I don't feel as though I'm doing very much here."

"You're just used to being the one charging around after the bad guys."

"And around you, my main job is trying to keep up."

He made it sound like a compliment, but Maya could also hear the uncertainty there, like he really wasn't sure whether he should be trying to hold her back a little.

"You're doing plenty," Maya assured him. "I need someone here who gets what's going on, and what's at stake. Besides, you're a good detective. You'll be able to spot things that I don't, and I definitely can't do all of this alone. If it's a choice between you and Reyes for backup, I'm choosing you."

Marco looked as though he might say something in response to that, but Tony the floor manager chose that moment to come back with a set of ledgers so large that it seemed that he could barely hold his arms out wide enough to hold them. There were several of them stacked atop one another, so that he had to keep them pinned in place with his chin, carrying them over to a table and setting them down.

"These ledgers contain copies of the original works from which William Hastel made his puzzles," Tony said. "All the ones that haven't been digitized yet. The pictures have a code next to them, saying which puzzle designs they were used with, so if you want, it should be possible to go through them and search for anything your puzzle pieces might match."

One look at the ledgers said to Maya that it would be slow, difficult work, yet Marco went over to them without her having to ask him, and Maya passed him the puzzle pieces to use as a point of comparison.

She watched as he opened the first ledger, it was big enough that it covered the whole table when it was opened fully, the paper within slightly yellowed and spotted with age. The first sheet was a full-page print of a portrait of a Victorian lady, presumably one that had been made into a puzzle at some point. Numbers at the side suggested which patterns it had been used for, while there were notes in a couple of neat copperplate hands that seemed to be some kind of technical shorthand to do with the printing process.

"I've got this," Marco assured her. "You work through the personnel list."

Maya nodded and went over to the other side of the room with Tony. She got out her tablet and used it to log into the FBI's systems, then typed in the first name on the list. She was looking for anyone who had a history of violence or instability, probably male, probably in their twenties or thirties. Statistically, the vast majority of serial killers fell into those categories. Still, she was going to run through all the names. She wanted to be thorough.

"Lucinda Adams?" Maya said to Tony.

"Artist. Produced a couple of pieces for us early in the year. Cats, if I remember right. No problems with anyone."

And no police record either. It seemed as if Tony really could remember everyone who'd worked there. Lucinda Adams didn't seem like a likely candidate, though, so Maya moved on to the next name.

"Simon Adrian?"

"A student who worked here before last Christmas. Always a busy period. He was late a few times, but mostly a good kid. Went back to college in January."

Meaning he wouldn't have been there at the time of Christine Weller's murder.

"Sophia Allen?"

"A machinist. Works with the 3D printers. Likes to get a little too drunk on a Friday night, couple of rumors about her and one of our artists having a relationship that meant she now refuses to work on anything Jim has designed, but nothing much."

One arrest, for drug possession while she was a teenager. Maya doubted that it was enough to point the finger at her.

She was impressed by how quickly Tony recalled the names she read out, giving Maya little precis of their working lives. It made for quicker going than reading through their HR files would have done, yet even so it was slow going. For every name, Maya had to check police records and the FBI's own systems, making sure that their names hadn't come up in connection with any serious crimes. Even with it taking only a minute or two per person, it was still going to take a long time to go through them all.

"How's it going over there?" Maya asked Marco, as he continued to work his way through the ledgers. He currently seemed to be pausing, holding the puzzle pieces up against one of the pages and rotating them, as if trying to work out where they fit.

"No, it's not this one. I thought it might be, but there are flowers here that don't fit with the water section."

"Keep going," Maya said. "You'll get it if it's there."

She believed that he would. Marco wasn't someone who gave up, and he had a good eye for detail that would soon spot any painting that the pieces would fit into. If they *did* find one, then it would be simply a matter of finding out who had ordered a copy in the last couple of years.

That might be manageable even if it wasn't possible to go through every custom order.

For now, though, there was the list of names to keep working through. The only trouble was that it didn't feel to Maya as if she was getting anywhere. It was another of those jobs that, in a normal investigation, she would have worked through diligently, whether it worked out or not, but now, was she just burning time she didn't have?

"Grant Durrell," Maya said, and instantly saw the difference in Tony the floor manager's expression. He looked as if he'd just bitten down on something sour. "What is it?"

"Oh, him," Tony said, with the same pained expression. There was definitely something more to this one employee than to the others.

"What about him?" Maya asked.

"He worked here for years," Tony said. "Got fired. He'd always been good at making the wrong kind of comments, maybe been a little too eager around some of our female staff."

Meaning that he'd harassed them, and no one had done anything about it. Even today, in a lot of companies, that seemed to be the way things were done.

"What got him fired?" Maya asked.

"Things turned… physical," Tony said, with obvious discomfort. "He crossed the line, got himself fired. Wasn't happy about it, as you can imagine."

"Did he make threats?" Maya asked.

"Well, we never took them seriously. You know how people can be when they're fired."

But he'd made threats. Maya typed his name into the FBI system, hardly daring to hope.

There on the system were more allegations in connection to harassing women, including a cease and desist for stalking one, a few years back.

Maya quickly used the FBI's systems to look at his social media. Most of it was public, so she'd didn't even have to put a call in to headquarters for access. She just scrolled back, reading as she went.

It was hard to ignore some of his posts. *If women dress like sluts, they shouldn't be surprised if men treat them that way*, was one that caught her eye. Another was, *Whether they admit it or not, all women secretly enjoy the feeling of being hunted.*

Given the state of social media, it might or might not mean anything. It might just be the kind of talk that some people engaged in to try to get attention. Even so, it was starting to paint a picture of the kind of man Grant Durrell was.

Then Maya saw a name that made her stop her scrolling. Trinity Dee was there, commenting on a couple of Durrell's posts. Arguing.

Shut up, bitch, unless you want me to shut you up.

In one reply, Grant Durrell had gotten Maya's full attention.

Maya kept scrolling, looking for any sign of Christine Weller. She couldn't see the teacher's name, but even so, the connection to one of the victims was undeniable. It was something to start with.

At the very least, it meant that she and Marco needed to ask Grant Durrell some questions.

CHAPTER FIFTEEN

Grant Durrell's place was an old house just outside of town, down several country lanes. Maya guessed that part of the reason he'd worked at Hastel's was that it was close by.

She could feel her tension rising as she and Marco drove down the lane towards the house. A sign warned against trespassing, but Maya ignored it. They needed to talk to Grant, and they weren't going to let that stop them.

The house was large, white painted, and slightly rickety looking, as if it hadn't been cared for in years. There were the shells of a couple of cars out in front of it, halfway rebuilt. As they pulled up, the place seemed quiet, but Maya wasn't about to believe that it was deserted that easily.

She led the way up to the front door. There was a screen across it, and Maya pulled it out of the way, ringing the doorbell. There was no answer. Maya rang it again, in case Grant simply hadn't heard.

There was still no answer.

"He's not here," Marco said. "We should go and come back later."

Maya knew that was what they ought to do. What they were *required* to do, in fact. Whatever else was going on, they were still officers of the law, which made what Maya was contemplating impossible.

"I want to get inside," Maya said.

She saw Marco's eyes widen.

"You know you can't do that, Maya," Marco said. "Without a warrant, you go in and any evidence you gather will be inadmissible."

"And if I don't go in, what then?" Maya demanded. "He gets away with this?"

"If it's him."

"A creepy guy with a history of harassing women, with a connection to the first victim, who *threatened* the first victim, who worked in the puzzle factory that probably produced the puzzle pieces that were left by the body."

"You think a judge will buy that?" Marco asked.

Maya knew he had a point. They needed more in the way of physical evidence, but how were they meant to get that physical evidence without access to Grant Durrell's place?

Maya made a call to her boss.

"Grey, how are things going over in Hastel?" he asked.

"I have a potential suspect, but I'm going to need a friendly judge if I'm going to get a warrant to search his house."

"How friendly? How speculative is this?"

Maya set out what she'd found as best she could. "There seems to be a connection to a games manufacturer here, because puzzle pieces were left both with Christine Weller's body and with another victim."

"Another victim? You're in town a day and already you've found a serial killer?"

She wasn't sure if Harris sounded impressed or exasperated.

"I think so," Maya replied. "I investigated at the manufacturer, and I've found a disgruntled former employee with a history of harassing women, who was fired when he got physical, and who made threats towards the first victim. Can you find a judge who will give me a warrant based on that?"

"I'll try," Harris said. "If they understand the stakes, there are one or two who might help. Maybe. Give me the address."

Maya texted him the name and address, and her boss hung up.

"You're doing the right thing," Marco said.

Only because he was there. Grant Durrell might be out there, plotting to kill another victim. That thought made her pace, wanting to be moving, wanting a chance to act. Now that Maya had thought of the possibility, it was impossible not to imagine Grant Durrell out there somewhere, stalking a victim, closing in on her because Maya was being too slow in catching up to him.

"It will be all right," Marco told her. "We still have the rest of the week. You're making progress."

If this were just about solving this before the deadline, that might have consoled her. As it was, though, the thought of Durrell possibly out there hunting someone else meant that she couldn't bring herself to stand still.

Finally, a call came back from Harris. Maya just had to hope that it was good news.

"Tell me you got the warrant," Maya said.

“You’re cleared to search the property,” Harris replied. “No warrant for an arrest yet, though. Not unless you find anything. And Grey? I hope you find something. This wasn’t easy to swing.”

He hung up, and Maya started towards the house.

“You got a warrant?” Marco asked.

Maya nodded. “It’s time to see what Grant Durrell is hiding in there.”

She made her way around the house, checking to see if there were any open doors or windows that would let her in easily. When Maya got to the back door of the house, she took out a set of lockpicks and started to work on the lock.

“I’m pretty sure that’s not standard FBI training,” Marco said.

“Military intelligence, remember?” Maya said. Sometimes, that had meant getting into places quietly, without leaving a trace. She’d learned to pick a lock for all the times when using C4 to blow it off its hinges wasn’t an option. It took her a minute, but the lock clicked open and she slipped inside.

She drew her weapon, because she didn’t know what kind of threats might be waiting for her in the house. Grant Durrell might be waiting in ambush, having decided to kill the people who had come to try to catch him. He might come out shooting, and Maya needed to be ready.

For the moment, though, the house appeared to be empty. The back door opened onto a kitchen where dishes were piled up in the sink, and the refrigerator hummed ominously loud against the silence of the house.

A small table sat at one end of the kitchen, with a pile of opened mail on it. Most of it looked like bills to Maya, nothing that would help to prove or disprove his involvement in all of this.

Marco was a pace behind her, gun also out and ready, backing her up. Maya was glad that she had someone with her who knew how to do that well, and who she knew wouldn’t freeze under fire, or do something stupid that might put them both in danger. Maya had always tried to avoid having a partner with her, because she didn’t want to have to spend her time looking after them, but she knew that Marco was more than capable of looking after himself.

She moved into what she assumed had started life as a dining room, but it was obvious that eating wasn’t its main purpose now. Instead, there were small tables set out around the room, and each one had a boardgame set out on it.

Maya hadn't seen any of them before, but that didn't mean much, given how few boardgames she'd played. Even so, there was a hand painted quality to most of them that suggested Grant Durrell had been making his own games here, or maybe taking home prototypes from work. There were boardgame covers and completed jigsaw puzzles stuck around the walls the way someone else might have put up paintings. The effect was a little overwhelming for Maya.

If people's homes were a reflection of who they were, what did this place say about Grant? What did her own almost empty apartment say about *her*?

"Does it look as though any of the puzzles here match the pieces we have?" Maya asked.

That was the first thing to check. It would also be her ideal scenario, with some kind of custom, one of a kind puzzle displayed prominently in a mocking declaration of Grant Durrell's guilt, as if anyone else would be too stupid to spot it. As Marco moved around the room, though, he shook his head.

"No, none of them match."

"So we move on," Maya said.

They made their way to the living room. This one had a single large armchair, suggesting that Durrell didn't get much in the way of company. More board games were set up around it, with a laptop on a small table in front of it and a few piles of books around the edges. Maya saw titles like *Monopoly: A Gaming History,* and *Everything You Need to Know About Clue*.

This was clearly a man who took his former job very seriously. Seriously enough that losing it had made something snap in him?

Maya wasn't sure. She needed more information, which meant that she and Marco needed to keep going through the house. They headed upstairs together, guns still sweeping ahead of them, checking for danger.

The landing they came to had four doors leading off. Maya tried the handle of the first, and found a bathroom. It hadn't been cleaned in a while, with grimy soap marks covering a lot of the surfaces. There was nothing there though that pointed to Grant Durrell being a murderer.

Maya moved on to the next room. It was a bedroom that seemed to have been converted to some kind of home office and workshop. There were small figurines on stands waiting to be painted. There was a desk on which papers were spread out, and Maya started to go through them, looking for anything that might be relevant to the case.

Then she turned back towards the door and saw it.

A cork board stood there, with photographs stuck to it. Each one was of a young woman, apparently taken with a long lens, from a distance. Some were taken through bedroom windows, of them half undressed, but others caught them in some ordinary, day to day moment, getting out of a car, or stepping out of an office.

"Shit," Marco said, as he looked at it all.

Maya nodded. This was a lot. This was… this was the kind of thing that a stalker might do, or someone planning something.

It was the kind of thing that a murderer might do while they were picking out a victim and trying to work out how to get to her.

Maya started to look through the photographs, looking for any sign of Christine Weller or Trinity Dee. Neither woman seemed to be in them, though. Did that mean that Durrell didn't have anything to do with them, or did he just keep his victims on the board while he was stalking them? Maybe, once he'd killed them, the photographs went somewhere else?

It would be stupid to keep them up there, after all.

She saw a couple of cameras sitting on a side table, along with a collection of lenses. They would need to take those for evidence.

Maya was about to keep searching when she heard a sound from downstairs: a door being opened.

She looked over at Marco, then gestured towards the door. In silence, she moved forward, wanting to get down there and see what was happening. She kept her weapon out, leading the way as the two of them headed downstairs.

A man stepped into their path. He was probably in his forties, lean and dark haired, wearing jeans, a plaid shirt and a denim jacket.

He also had a gun, a bulky looking .45 that he pointed Maya's way.

"Freeze!" he yelled. "Move and I'll blow your head off!"

"Drop your weapon," Maya ordered him, keeping her Glock levelled at him. She knew without having to look that Marco would have his own weapon trained on the newcomer.

"*You* drop your weapon," he replied. "If you think I'm giving in to some kind of home invasion…"

Maya had to fight the instinct to fire as he kept the weapon pointing her way. The truth was that there was no transition between pointing a gun and pulling the trigger. If he decided to do it, there wouldn't be enough time to react. The safe thing would be to fire now. All her training called for it, but she forced herself to stop.

"This isn't a home invasion," Maya said. "I'm FBI, and we have a warrant."

She half expected him to start shooting, realizing just how much danger of discovery he was in. Maya had already decided that, with no cover on the stairs, her only option was to throw herself forward down them and fire back, hoping that the sudden movement made him miss.

"FBI?" he made no move to attack, which caught Maya a little by surprise.

"I have my ID in my pocket," Maya said. "I'm going to reach for it slowly."

She took it out, not taking her eyes off him, and then tossed the ID to him. Durrell caught it clumsily, and in that moment, if Maya had wanted to, she could have taken him down without the risk of him firing back.

Instead, she waited while he read it. The moment he did, his features paled, and his gun went clattering out of his hands, falling to the floor. Maya hurried forward, grabbing for him and wrenching his arms behind his back. Marco kept his gun trained on Durrell while Maya cuffed him one handed.

"Grant Durrell," she said. "You're under arrest."

CHAPTER SIXTEEN

Marco couldn't help admiring Maya as they sat opposite Grant Durrell in a Hastel PD interrogation room, trying to work out the best way to get into his head. In moments like this, he could see the intelligence and determination that had first started to attract him to her all the way back in Cleveland.

And the fact that she was an attractive woman in general, of course.

Not that it had been that long, a few weeks at most since he'd first met her. Yet somehow, in that time, it had come to feel as though he'd known Maya forever. It was a big part of the reason he was here, even when his boss said that he shouldn't be.

Marco was sure that there would be plenty of messages waiting for him from Chief Linden on his phone. He clearly wasn't happy about this leave of absence, even if he hadn't actually fired Marco yet. Marco ignored that thought, for now. He and Maya had a killer to catch.

He hoped they'd already caught him.

Grant Durrell was currently holding a whispered conversation with his lawyer on one side of a cheap wooden table set between them and Maya. A recording device sat in the middle, and a camera monitored things from the corner.

Marco waited at the edge of the room, standing by the door, not saying anything for now. He knew that Maya had this, and he could jump in if she needed him. At least here, like this, he could add to an air of mild intimidation that might encourage Durrell to talk.

Maya *didn't* seem inclined to talk, not yet. Instead, she was setting down pictures one by one on the table, turning them so that Durrell could see them. She waited several seconds, just letting him stare at them. Marco could admire the psychology of that, giving Durrell time in which to think of everything that the two of them might already know. With all the charging around after bad guys, it was easy to forget how good Maya was at this side of things as well.

"Tell us why these photographs were in your house," Maya said.

"I like pictures of good-looking women," Durrell said, in a tone that almost made a joke of it. "I have lady friends. I take pictures of them."

"With a long lens?" Maya said. "Taken when they're getting out of cars or going into their houses? Those aren't the kind of intimate pictures people take, Grant."

"What my client does in his private life is hardly a police matter, Agent Grey," Durrell's lawyer said.

"Except when he's stalking women, ready to kill them," Marco put in from his corner of the room. He knew his cue when he heard it.

"Kill them?" Grant said. Marco saw the shock on his face at those words, but he'd seen plenty of people pretending innocence in interrogations before. "What is this?"

"This is where you start telling the truth, Grant," Maya said. "Where you stop pretending that you got the permission of these women to photograph them."

"I did," Grant said. "Ok, I got some of them from the internet, too, but…"

"When I take these photographs for analysis," Maya said. "Do you think that the FBI's tech guys will say that the photographs came from the internet? Or do you think they'll tell me that they were all taken with one camera, from a distance?"

"My client has already explained that," the lawyer said. To Marco, it sounded like a pretty weak attempt.

Maya obviously thought so too. "What are their names, Grant? Shall we start with that? And once you've given me their names, we can move on to how I contact them, so I can ask each one if they really gave you the permission that you're claiming. It will take time, and I hate having my time wasted, but I will do it if I have to, with every single one."

Marco could see how uncomfortable Durrell looked at being caught in the lie like that.

"Or you could just admit that you've been stalking them," Maya said. "We know how you feel about women. I've seen your social media feeds. I've heard how things ended for you over at Hastel's."

"What does my job have to do with anything?" Durrell shot back. Marco could hear the flash of anger there. It seemed that Maya had found a way to get an honest response out of him.

"I think it has a lot to do with things," Maya said. "It was clearly your life. I've seen the inside of your home. Puzzles and games are everything for you."

"I like them," Durrell said.

"You're obsessed with them," Maya countered. Marco could appreciate her not giving their suspect time to think. It was important to keep momentum at this point. "You had your dream job, working at a company that let you work with your hobby, and that also didn't care too much when you harassed some of the female employees there."

"I never harassed anyone," Durrell said. "They *wanted* me to-"

"Did any of them say that?" Maya asked. "Or did you just decide they wanted your attentions? That's what got you fired, isn't it?"

Marco saw another flash of anger go through Durrell. Maya was obviously provoking him, trying to get him to show the kind of man he really was.

"I got fired because the company went all corporate. I still do ok, making games freelance."

"I'm more interested in how angry you were at getting fired," Maya said. Somehow, she still sounded calm. "Angry enough to push you over the edge? Angry enough that you took it out on Trinity Dee and Christine Weller?"

"Who?" Durrell asked.

Maya was already shaking her head. "That doesn't work, Grant. I know you and Trinity were in contact online. I know you know who she was. I know you made threats towards her. When I start going through your cameras, am I going to find pictures of you stalking her, gathering information, getting ready to murder her?"

"I haven't murdered anybody!" Durrell snapped back. "I don't even know who Christine Weller is."

Maya went silent then, and Marco got the impression that she was trying to get a read on Durrell, attempting to decide how much of the truth he was telling.

"She *was* a teacher," Maya said. "A good person, murdered here, the same way that Trinity Dee was. By the same person. I have evidence that links the murders to the Hastel factory, where I found a former employee who harasses women, and who has a connection to at least one of the dead women. A former employee who keeps photographs of women that he's taken from a distance, like he's working out the best way to kill them."

"No, that's not true," Durrell said. "You're twisting things."

Marco saw Maya turn to him. "Marco, we got the cameras from his house, right?"

Marco nodded. "We have them. You want me to look through them?"

"Please. If there's any picture of Christine or Trinity, find it." She looked back to Durrell. "Will he find one, Grant?"

"No, of course not! I don't *do* anything to these women. I just… I just take pictures."

It was possible that there wouldn't be, but even so, Marco needed to check. More than that, he needed to know if there was anything else. Marco went back to the office he and Maya had been given, taking the cameras and starting to work his way through their hard drives.

He learned a lot about Grant Durrell's obsessions pretty quickly. There was picture after picture of women there, all between about twenty and forty, most photographed multiple times. This wasn't someone who just grabbed a quick picture whenever he thought he could get away with it.

Marco saw one sequence of photographs featuring a young woman with high cheekbones and brightly dyed hair that seemed to change almost from shot to shot. There was one of her meeting up with a group of friends, one of her getting into a taxi, one of her coming out of an apartment building, and then a whole series of shots taken through its windows, including a couple of her having sex with different people. That was creepy enough, but the one of her sleeping on her couch was worse, somehow, even more of an intrusion. It was the kind of thing that made Marco feel a deep sense of disgust when it came to Grant Durrell.

A part of him wanted to march into the interrogation room and punch the other man, but he had to keep looking through the photographs anyway, trying to find any trace of the two murder victims. Marco wasn't expecting a full sequence of photographs for them, but just one that Durrell had forgotten to get rid of would be enough.

It occurred to Marco as he looked through the photographs that there was a possible way to narrow things down. Each photograph had an automatic date and time stamp in the corner, easy to remove when Durrell was printing them out, but more than useful for Marco now.

He knew the dates of the two murders, so all he had to do was look for photographs taken in the lead up. It meant that he could hurry through sequences of photographs without having to look at every detail of Durrell's obsession. Marco had seen plenty of things that would keep most people awake, but there was something genuinely disturbing about the way this creep had simply… watched women.

Or maybe not simply watched. There was a good chance that he'd done far more than that to Trinity Dee and Christine Weller. Marco just had to find the proof.

Marco kept looking through the photographs, trying to find the correct dates. He got closer, and now he had to scour every photograph, making sure that neither of the victims appeared in any of them. Just one shot that had them, even on an edge, would be enough to prove a connection.

Then Marco reached the date of Christine Weller's murder, and saw the photographs. He understood in an instant what they meant.

He hurried back to the interrogation room, not bothering to knock before he burst in.

"Did you find something?" Maya asked, looking up at him as he entered with hope.

"Come outside, you need to see this."

Maya followed him outside, leaving Durrell and his lawyer to confer.

"What is it, Marco? What did you find?"

"Look," Marco said, pulling up the photographs from the date of Christine Weller's murder.

There were a lot, a whole sequence of a young woman, maybe twenty-five, obviously taken through the windows of her house. Durrell had pictures of her eating, of her making phone calls, of her in the shower…

"What am I looking at, Marco?" Maya asked.

"Look at the time stamps," Marco said.

He saw Maya look, and the change in her expression was instant, the disappointment spreading as quickly as a storm as she started to understand the point of what Marco was showing her.

"There are no photographs of the victims, but, in the whole time period when Christine Weller could have been killed, he was outside this woman's house, taking photographs," Marco said.

Maya's expression was flat with disappointment. "Meaning that it couldn't have been him who killed her."

"There are photographs on the same date Trinity Dee died as well." Marco made an apology of it, because he'd wanted this to be Grant

Durrell as much as Maya had. "He's not our killer, just an asshole with a camera."

Maya looked as though she wanted to punch something in that moment. Marco could understand the feeling.

"We can hold him for the stalking, at least," she said. "But it's not enough. It means we've wasted most of today chasing after him, when we could have been out gathering other leads. I *hate* getting things wrong."

Marco did his best to reassure her. He'd seen how capable Maya was, but also how easily she could spiral when things started to go wrong. "You followed the evidence where it led. There wasn't anything else you could do, Maya. He looked like a good suspect."

"But not the right one." Maya shook her head. "We need to find new evidence now, and if we don't do it soon…"

Marco understood the stakes. If they didn't do it soon, then a woman's life hung in the balance. They had to find another lead, and soon.

CHAPTER SEVENTEEN

He watched her through the crowd on Hastel's main street, hanging back and making sure that she couldn't see him.

She looked no older now than she did in his mind's eye, in her thirties, even though he was older now. She still had the same dark hair, still had that slender physique and that natural, fine-boned beauty that had always made it hard to look away from her, in spite of what she'd done.

That thought made him want to walk up to her and scream at her, right there in the middle of the crowd. There was a time when he might even have done it, but he held back now. Seeing him do that might give people too much of a clue, when he did what he had to do.

He *thought* he'd done it before. He thought that he'd taken care of this, expunged the demons of the past, but no; somehow, she was still there in front of him, taunting him just by being there.

She was talking to some guy at the moment. Not her husband, because he knew her husband almost as well as he knew her. There wasn't the same hate inside him for the husband, though. He hadn't done what she had. His crime had been one of absence, not all the things she'd done.

He walked closer, and he knew that he should at least pretend to look into the stores on either side, pretend that he was out there in the town so that he could spend the day shopping, or visiting the puzzle museum, or whatever it was people did while they were out here. He should look away from her, and keep track of her only in glances.

He couldn't take his eyes off her, though, couldn't look away, in spite of everything. *Because* of everything. There was something about cruelty that made it into almost as great an attractive force as love.

Not that he really knew about love. He'd tried, of course, because he'd heard that was people wanted from life, but it had never quite worked out for him. No matter how much he pretended, somehow, women always sensed something broken in him, something wrong. He could manage friendships, or at least the *illusion* of friendships, because even with those, he couldn't let people get too close.

He was broken, and she was the one who had broken him. She left him with a piece missing, like a jigsaw puzzle that could never be finished.

He had to make that right. Had to do something about the feelings that wouldn't go away. He kept moving forward, his eyes so focused on her now that he almost bumped into people as he walked past them. Only the instinct to avoid attracting attention kept him from pushing people out of the way in order to get closer to her.

She was still talking to the man, laughing at something he'd said, acting as if she didn't have a care in the world. The two of them stepped apart, with the man going one way and her going the other.

He kept following her. He had no interest in anyone else.

Now, though, he *did* bump into someone, feeling his shoulder slam into theirs. He found himself facing a big guy, whose face twisted into an automatic kind of anger.

"Hey, watch where you're going!"

"Sorry, sorry," he said. He didn't want trouble, certainly didn't want some kind of fight. He wasn't a violent man. He only did what he had to do in order to make the pain of what she'd done stop.

"We got some kind of problem?" the guy demanded.

"No, no, sorry," he said, moving on as quickly as he could. It was important to keep moving, keep getting closer, keep watching the only woman in all of this who mattered. The face he couldn't get out of his mind.

He was very close now, close enough that if he'd wanted to, he could have taken out a weapon and killed her there and then. A part of him wanted to do it, wanted to just kill her there in the street and shout out everything she'd done to him to deserve it.

That wouldn't be the best way to do it, though. This was something personal, something *private*.

In any case, he didn't want to be caught doing this. He didn't want to be sent to jail for it. She'd already taken so much from him; he wasn't going to let her take the rest of his life as well.

He was so close now that he could meet her eyes. She looked at him, eyes moving over him as if trying to decide whether he was familiar or not. He froze in place in that moment, sure that she would recognize him, half-hoping that she might.

What would she do if she did realize who he was? Sometimes, in his dreams, he stood in front of her while she apologized for everything she'd done. He stood there and listened to her pour out her heart, telling him how sorry she was, and somehow taking away the pain.

In real life, he suspected that it wasn't that easy. Even if she did apologize, then it wouldn't make anything better. It wouldn't change what she'd done, or all the ways that it had ruined his life in the years since.

He would still have to kill her.

Besides, she would never apologize. She'd always insisted that she was right, that she was doing the right thing. She'd never cared about the harm she was doing to him.

She was still looking at him, but he realized that it was because he was looking at her. She smiled slightly, then looked away, as if that was all he was worth, all he meant. Didn't she even remember him? Didn't she remember what she'd done? Or did she just care about it that little?

Whatever the answer, it didn't matter. What mattered was that he'd found her. He'd found her, and soon, she would pay. He wouldn't do it here, wouldn't do it where he might be caught, but he'd found her now.

Soon, he would kill her for everything she'd done.

CHAPTER EIGHTEEN

Even after the failure with Grant Durrell, Maya was convinced that puzzles were still at the heart of this. It was the only thing she still had to go on, now that Grant Durrell definitely wasn't the killer. The only question was how to use that.

Marco was currently sitting across the office from her, going through more images of Hastel's puzzles, trying to find a match. Nothing so far seemed to have even come close, though, so Maya found herself worrying that they might use up all the time they had on that, when they needed to be out there, finding new leads.

"This town is filled with boardgame obsessives," Maya said. "There should be *some* other way that we can find out more about the puzzle pieces that were left, and about the kind of person who would leave pieces at a crime scene."

"Leaving puzzle pieces definitely feels like someone connected to that community," Marco said.

Community. That was the important word there. This wasn't a collection of isolated individuals. Maya had seen for herself at the games store that all of this was more than just an individual pursuit, and Grant Durrell's house had made it clear that it was more than just a hobby for some people.

Somewhere in that community, there would be someone who could tell her more.

"I want to find more games people," Maya said. "The only way into all of this is if we find people who can tell us more."

Getting out her computer, she started looking for more game stores, but that didn't feel right. She didn't want to just go from store to store in case she simply happened on one where someone could give her an answer. There had to be a better way.

Maya searched for puzzle forums instead online, and the only problem with *that* was the sheer number of them that she found. Millions of people played boardgames and made puzzles. Maya needed to find ways to narrow it down a little.

Puzzles, Hastel.

That search got her the official site of the Hastel Games Company, but also a bunch of threads talking about it, pages on its history, reviews of its productions, blogposts by people using its products, and far more. Maya scrolled through the list until she spotted something that looked particularly promising.

There, in the middle of the search list, Maya spotted a thread given over to Hastel's old puzzles. She saw pictures of completed ones, and recreations of half-forgotten ones. There was a whole complex argument about trying to piece together one where the records seemed to have been lost, using descriptions in a couple of obscure hundred-year-old letters.

Maya hadn't known that the records *could* be lost. She'd thought that the ledgers were all the ones there were. What did that mean for her hopes of finding the puzzle? What if it was something from one of those lost ledgers?

And there were threads where people attempted to identify puzzles from only a few parts of them. Some seemed to be a kind of game in itself, testing their knowledge. Others seemed to be genuine attempts to work out what a partially surviving puzzle might have looked like.

An idea came to Maya, although it wasn't one that she would normally have contemplated. If she hadn't already shown the jigsaw pieces at the games store, she wouldn't have considered it at all. But she had, and there was no denying that when it came to Hastel puzzle pieces, these were the experts.

Maya took photographs of the puzzle pieces and sent them to the thread.

I know it's a long shot, but can anyone identify the puzzle these came from? I found the pieces recently, and now I really want to see the whole picture.

She left out the fact that it was for the FBI. It seemed more likely to get help, that way. These were the kind of people who might balk at helping the government, but who might try to help her just for the challenge of it.

Looks like pattern H3156 to me, Puzzlefanatic31 wrote back after a minute or so, *but it's hard to tell the actual pattern.*

Maybe 'Flowing Chrysanthemums'? Iknowpuzzles12 suggested.

Then where are the chrysanthemums?

A picture showed up on the screen. For a moment, Maya's heart raced in anticipation, but as she tried to match the pieces to it, they simply didn't fit.

That's an H546 anyway, RossisGreat wrote. *Don't be stupid.*

Don't call me stupid, you're stupid.

It went downhill from there, and Maya winced as she realized that it wasn't likely to get any better in a hurry.

"Trouble?" Marco asked.

"I think I've started a flame war."

Worse, there wasn't any sign that anyone knew their puzzle. Maya was just about to sign off in disgust when she noticed something under a thread marked "Events."

Hastel Puzzle Contest.

Maya checked the date. It was tonight. Tonight, there would be dozens of the most competitive puzzle solvers out there in the town, all in one place. If anyone could identify the puzzle pieces, they would be there. And if anyone was likely to know someone so obsessed with puzzles that they left them behind when they killed, it was another obsessive puzzle solver.

Perhaps the killer would even be in attendance.

"Marco, I think I've found where we need to go next."

*

The first thing that caught Maya's attention was the scale of the hall. It was bigger than she might have expected. She'd thought that this would be some small-scale event, with a few enthusiasts gathered around to compete against one another. Instead, there were dozens of them, so that even a hall big enough to hold a theatre production felt full.

The second thing was the hushed quiet of it all. It was like being in a library, or the middle of an examination. Indeed, it looked a lot like an examination, too, with each competitor sitting at an individual table, a felt board spread out on it as they worked to assemble the pieces of a puzzle set in front of them. There were clocks beside them, counting the seconds that it took to complete each puzzle, and even as she watched, Maya saw a hand slap down on one of those clocks, the puzzler's hands then going up in the air as if to demonstrate that they weren't touching anything else.

She saw a figure go over, looking down at the puzzle, then raising a small green flag. Maya guessed that was a theatrical touch for the spectators, but it had never occurred to her that there would even *be* spectators to need that kind of element.

Then again, until today, she hadn't even guessed that this kind of competitive puzzle solving existed. Jigsaw puzzles had seemed like a solitary pursuit, something to take one's time with and put together peacefully, not scramble furiously to construct correctly while clocks and arbiters looked on.

"How do you want to do this?" Marco asked, looking over the room. Maya could tell he thought the whole event as strange as she did.

"You have pictures of the pieces?" Maya asked.

He nodded, holding up his phone.

"Right here."

"Then I think we'll cover more ground if we split up. Ask around and see if anyone has seen them before. Also, see if the names of the victims mean anything to anyone here."

Marco smiled. "I know what to do, don't worry."

Ordinarily, that was a phrase that would only have made Maya worry more, thinking about all the things that someone else might miss while she wasn't there to ask the questions herself. With Marco, though, she found that she felt confident that he would do a good job, leaving her free to concentrate on her own half of it.

It was such a strange feeling, having a partner she knew she could trust. One who actually had her back.

Maya set off into the hall, walking around the tables and trying to get a sense of the people there. There was a mix of men and women of all ages there, even a few kids looking on as if the whole thing were the most exciting thing they'd seen in a while.

Briefly it even occurred to her that, if the killer truly was a puzzle obsessive, he might be here, watching.

Maya had to admit that it was impressive, the speed at which some of them were placing pieces. There was no leisurely assessment of which pieces might go with which others, which might be a corner or an edge. There was instead a mad scramble to get everything in place.

She saw another clock slapped, another pair of hands going up. This time though, the arbiter raised a red flag, Maya assumed to signal that some piece was slightly out of place. She heard the whole audience around her give a kind of collective groan at it.

Maya kept moving through them, trying to work out who might be able to help her. She approached one of the arbiters standing at the side, getting out her ID and tapping him on the shoulder.

"Excuse me, I-"

"Sorry, I need to focus."

Maya hadn't heard anyone sound that serious when there weren't about to be bullets flying. It certainly didn't seem to fit with someone watching other people put puzzles together. Even when she brought her ID up for him to see, he didn't look over at it.

Maybe this wasn't the person to ask.

Maya headed into the audience instead, and realized that anyone there to watch this would probably know something about puzzles. Maya approached a trio who appeared to be a couple of parents with their young boy.

"Excuse me," she said. She showed her ID.

"The FBI are here?" the man said. "What is it? Afraid that drug cartels are smuggling using puzzles now?"

He laughed at it, and Maya made herself laugh along.

"Not quite that," Maya said, with a glance towards the kid. She really didn't want to go into the full details of what was happening with him there. She didn't really want to go into the details of a serial killer at all, come to that. "I just need someone who can help me to identify a couple of jigsaw pieces."

"I know lots of puzzles," the boy said. "I've been learning them!"

"Learning them?" Maya said, not quite understanding.

The woman explained it. "For this kind of competition, it helps if you know the puzzles in advance. If they give you one you've seen, or where you know the manufacturer's pattern, you can put them together quicker."

That made a kind of sense. It just took a moment or two for Maya to wrap her mind around the idea that people trained for puzzle competitions. Was there enough money or prestige in them to really justify that? It felt as though there was this whole world that she didn't know anything about.

Maya showed them photographs of the pieces.

"Just those?" the man said.

"Yes."

Both parents looked over to their son. He shook his head.

"No, I haven't seen it."

"You're sure?" Maya said.

He nodded with a certainty that made Maya wonder just how much time he spent memorizing.

"Do you think someone else might know?" Maya asked.

"Maybe one of the main competitors," the woman said, gesturing to a corner where half a dozen men and women stood in a group, not competing yet.

"Main competitors?" Maya said. She nodded to the competition in front of her. "*This* isn't the main competition?"

"Oh no, this is the open category," the man said. "People do a single puzzle at their own pace. Those are doing the advanced category. Two puzzles at once, so they can mix up pieces, and they still go faster than the fastest people here."

"They're the fastest," the young boy said, with the kind of admiration that another young man might have reserved for some major sports star.

"Two puzzles at once?" Maya asked. Even as she said it, an announcer walked up to a stage at the front, where six individual tables sat, along with a couple of screens that seemed to be designed to show the action from the top down.

"Ladies and gentlemen, the time has come for our main competition," the announcer said, as the six competitors showed themselves to their seats. A plain box sat in front of each one, presumably filled with the mixed pieces of two puzzles.

"Our competitors will simultaneously assemble two puzzles that they haven't seen, until now," the announcer said. He moved over to two easels set near the front of the stage, placing large pieces of card on them. He peeled off what had to be a layer of white plastic, revealing pictures beneath. One appeared to be a van Gogh painting, while the other was of a large red windmill. "Five hundred pieces each. Are you all ready?"

For the first time since Maya had come into the room, there was noise, as people cheered.

"Then let's begin!" the announcer said, and blew a whistle.

CHAPTER NINETEEN

Maya had thought that there was a kind of quiet intensity to the general puzzle competition, but this was something on another level entirely. The whole competition below had ground to a halt while everyone stared at the stage at the front of the hall.

At least, they stared at the screens set to either side. From where she was standing, there was no way that Maya could make out the pictures being constructed under the hands of the puzzlers, and she assumed that was true for the majority of the people in the hall. There was only what she could see on the screens.

She guessed that most of the people were here for the atmosphere of it as much as to see what action there was. There seemed to be a kind of tension in the room that Maya might have associated with the final moments of some major sporting event, or maybe even with the build up to a raid, yet all that was happening was people putting together jigsaw puzzles.

On the screens at the front, puzzles started to fly together. Maya guessed that doing two at once was much more difficult than one at a time, because there was the additional problem of trying to sort the pieces into one puzzle or another.

"How hard is it to do this?" Maya asked the parents of the small boy.

"Two at once is hard," the boy said. "I tried, but you can't just go by shape. You can't just memorize the patterns."

He said that in the intense tones of someone who wished that he were able to do it. Maya wondered again just how much time he spent learning puzzle patterns by rote.

Up on the screens, Maya saw competitors sorting pieces into one pattern or another, picking them out by color and shape, fitting them together with a speed that seemed almost impossible to her.

Even among them, one participant seemed to be moving faster than any of the others. He was a man in his thirties, skinny and dark haired, wearing clothes that seemed a little too formal for the setting in the form of a full three-piece suit.

The pieces on his felt board seemed almost to put themselves together; he was moving that quickly. He seemed to be focusing with an incredible degree of intensity, eyes lasering in on the pieces as he worked.

He seemed to be focusing on one puzzle at a time while the others were going from one to another, the van Gogh almost finished already.

"Who's that?" Maya asked the boy, and it seemed strange that in this context, such a small boy was the closest thing she could find to an expert.

"That's Tommy Briner," the boy said, as if it were something that everyone should know. "He's a superstar. I watch all his YouTube videos."

YouTube videos for puzzlers? Stars in this tiny field that Maya hadn't heard anything about before? Maya guessed that it was possible, because it happened with almost every other field of human endeavor. Why *not* puzzles?

Even so, the notion of a puzzler being a superstar was a lot to get her mind around.

Maya could get some of it, seeing the intensity of the concentration there on his face. She could imagine someone watching that level of concentration and getting something out of it. She could definitely hear the near hero worship in the young man's voice.

Maya could also understand a little bit of how difficult this must be, even if she didn't entirely understand this as a competition. She could get that this took skills of pattern recognition and being able to see connections; after all, those were the most important skills in her own work. She knew, though, that she wouldn't appreciate all the nuances of all this. With anything, it tended to be only the people near the top level who could truly appreciate the genius of those at the very top.

In that instant, Maya found herself thinking about the Moonlight Killer.

Tommy had the first puzzle together completely now, and was starting work on the second, starting to put together the windmill from the base up at a speed that made it seem as though he already knew where all of the pieces should go, and it was just a case of physically getting them there.

Was one of the reasons the Moonlight Killer was doing all of this because he wanted Maya to be an audience to what he saw as his brilliance? Did he feel as if Maya was the only person in a position to truly appreciate the complexity of his crimes, that only someone who was catching other killers for him could truly understand how expertly planned his own murders were?

Up on the stage, Tommy seemed to have the second puzzle together by now, except for a couple of pieces. Everyone else still seemed to have most of their puzzles still to complete, so that it was as if there were two competitions: one with all of them, and one with just him. Maya had to remind herself that this was the top table, reserved for the best people there.

And he was still ahead of them all. Again, Maya had the impression of the Moonlight Killer trying to prove how much better he was than all his imitators. Was this what all of this was about?

Maya saw Tommy pick up the last of the pieces with a flourish and place it down in one of the remaining two spaces. Maya thought that there was an almost audible click as he set it into place, and she could see triumph there on his face even from a distance.

Then his expression changed. Maya saw a flicker of worry flash across his features, and now all the cameras were on him, blowing it all up on the screens set beside the stage. She saw his eyes darting around, almost frantically now.

Maya realized that he couldn't find the final piece.

The crowd seemed to realize it in the same moment, starting to murmur.

The picture was perfect, except for one piece missing from it, standing out like a lost tooth in a smile. The emptiness stood there, accusing in its incompleteness, and Maya could see just how much that lack was getting to Tommy. He was looking everywhere, eyes scanning the table, looking under it and around it, as if the missing piece would suddenly appear in front of him. As if it were just a blind spot, and if he just looked hard enough, it would magically appear in his vision.

The murmurs from the crowd were getting louder now. They'd realized that something was going badly wrong.

Meanwhile, the puzzles of the others were starting to catch up, getting more complete by the moment. One of them had the van Gogh finished now, and was more than halfway through the windmill.

Tommy was up out of his chair now, looking around under the table as if he might have dropped it. Maya guessed that would be the most likely place for it to be. Maybe he'd knocked it while getting the pieces out of the box, sending one of them falling to the floor. Maybe he would find it down there, snatch it up, and still have enough time to get it into place and win. Maybe this would turn into the kind of last-minute victory that Maya associated with sports movies.

Then the first of the competitors there slapped their clock to show that they were finished. An arbiter came over, raised a flag, and just like that, Tommy Briner had lost when he should have won.

One by one, as Tommy continued to search under the table, the others started to hit their clocks, and the arbiters came over to confirm that they'd completed them correctly. As the final flag went up, Maya realized that the favorite had come in last place. It was over.

Then, a few seconds later, it was clear to Maya that it wasn't, because Tommy Briner wasn't giving up. He was still searching beneath the table, hand flailing this way and that as if he might locate it by touch. He stood up sharply, looking around this way and that as if he couldn't understand why it wasn't there.

He went up to another of the competitors, towering over them since the others were still seated.

"Did you steal it?" he demanded, and he sounded more panicked than angry. He turned to another. "Did you?"

Now he *did* sound angry. He sounded as if he genuinely believed that someone had attempted to sabotage him by taking one piece out of the box. He started to shove tables out of the way, obviously looking for the missing piece, but the movement just meant that one of his competitor's puzzles fell to the ground, pieces scattering everywhere.

Tommy knelt among the pieces, searching through them, obviously still looking for the one that he was missing.

"He can't do this," one of his competitors insisted in a loud voice. "I don't care if it's Tommy Briner, he can't *do* this."

One of the arbiters, a woman in her forties wearing a high visibility jacket and a lanyard, stepped forward.

"That's enough," she said. "It's over."

"It's *not over*!" Tommy yelled, standing up in front of her. "I have to finish it!"

"It's done," the arbiter said. "You lost. The sets are triple checked, and the rules clearly state that if a player loses a piece, that's on them."

Tommy seemed to be rocking back and forth in place then, with the tension that was running through him. Tommy wasn't looking at her now. He was looking down at the floor, at the pieces lying there. He crouched there, trying to sort through them again, looking for that one piece.

Maya saw the arbiter crouch beside him, putting a hand on his shoulder.

"The competition is done."

He jerked back, stood, and then did one thing that echoed around the room. He slapped the arbiter, hard. The crack of it was sharp enough that Maya could guess how much it stung. The arbiter stumbled back, a couple of the players catching her to stop her from falling.

Tommy started forward, and a couple of the other arbiters got in the way, blocking him from getting close. Tommy flailed at them without any real skill, but now they were fighting, and it was hard to keep track of the punches being thrown.

Maya looked around at the rest of the room. She realized that, aside from her and Marco, there were no law enforcement officers there. Which meant that it fell to her to deal with this.

She hurried forward, pushing through the crowd, hoping that she could get there before this turned into some kind of major fight. She held her ID out in front of her as if it could push people out of her way, and most of them did fall back to let her through.

"FBI, let me up there!" Maya shouted as a couple of spectators got in the way.

She saw Marco approaching from the other side, forcing his way up onto the stage.

The two of them reached the fight at the same time, and Maya pulled the arbiter nearest to her away from Tommy. Marco did the same with another. Tommy was clear for a moment, and Maya could see the bruises rising on his face now. He fell to the floor, hunting among the puzzle pieces, and Maya had to step in the way as one of the arbiters looked as though he was lining up a punch.

"Don't," Maya warned, and maybe it was her tone, but the man backed off instantly.

She saw Marco push another couple of men back, then start towards Tommy. Maya shook her head. She suspected that would only spark more violence. She left it for a moment, and Tommy's hand came out of the pile with a puzzle piece. He went over to his table, and set it slowly, almost lovingly, into position.

Now, Maya moved in with Marco.

"Tommy?" she said.

He seemed to ignore her.

"Tommy?"

He rounded on her then. Apparently, any interruption was enough. He raised his hand, but Maya was quicker, moving into him and grabbing him. She ducked under his arm, got behind him, and started to work to wrench his arms behind his back.

Tommy howled with it, fighting and bucking. If Marco hadn't been there, Maya wasn't sure that she could have controlled the sheer random violence of his flailing. As it was, though, they managed to get his hands behind his back, so that Maya could cuff him.

Even then, he was still fighting, and it took Maya a moment to realize why. Carefully, she reached out and hit his clock to stop it. Tommy went still almost as soon as she did it.

"Tommy Briner, you're under arrest."

CHAPTER TWENTY

Maya left Tommy Briner in an interrogation room to calm down a little before she talked to him. It would give him time for his lawyer to get there, and in any case, she wanted to do a little research on the puzzler before she spoke to him.

"We could leave this to local PD," Marco said. "It's just an assault case, and we need to spend all our time looking into the murder."

Maya got why he might say it. At first glance, this did look as if she were wasting time that the two of them simply didn't have; yet some instinct made Maya want to look closer.

After all, they were looking for someone in the puzzle world who had the capacity for violence. Maybe Tommy Briner was a good place to start.

"I want to take a closer look at him," Maya said. "A guy *that* obsessed with puzzles, who has just shown that he doesn't mind lashing out?"

"Are you saying that he's a candidate to be our killer?" Marco asked.

Maya knew that it was a stretch, yet it was obvious that Tommy was in Hastel at least some of the time, was potentially violent, and was strongly connected to puzzles.

"I don't know," Maya said. "But I want to at least check out the possibility."

Maya started by running his name through the police systems. Almost instantly, a record came up, showing multiple arrests. Some had been for causing a public disturbance, others had been for assault. What was strange though was that there never seemed to be any charges filed.

Maya started to look into him deeper. She checked out his social media channels, and there were plenty of videos there of him solving puzzles, but Maya was more interested in a couple of the other videos that showed up when she typed in his name.

One had the title "Another Tommy Briner Meltdown," and showed him halfway through solving a puzzle in what appeared to be a restaurant with people all around him.

Maya saw the moment when one of the waiters approached, and accidentally knocked his puzzle, sending pieces scattering. Tommy was on his feet in an instant, shouting obscenities. A second or two after that, he flipped over the table. A moment after *that*, he threw a punch.

Maya clicked on another video, entitled "Tommy Briner goes too far with fellow puzzler," and this one cut in right as an argument was escalating. A man Maya assumed to be the fellow puzzler of the title was shouting and pushing his way into Tommy's space, apparently in the middle of some kind of convention. Seeming satisfied, he turned to walk away.

Maya saw the cold, calculating look come over Tommy, so she wasn't surprised when she saw him pick up a chair from a nearby stall and hit the other puzzler from behind, knocking him sprawling.

"He really does have a violent streak," Marco said.

"I'm more interested in the pause *before* he hit the other guy in that one," Maya replied. "In the first one, and today, it was violent acting out, just an immediate reaction. In that one, *he* seemed like the calm one, then he just decided to hit the other guy. Like Tommy had decided that he was a problem, and had to solve it."

"You're wondering if he ever had any cause to think of Christine Weller or Trinity Dee as problems?" Marco asked.

It was still a big jump from acting out violently to deciding to kill two people, yet Maya felt as though she at least had to ask the question.

She headed over to the interrogation room and found that Tommy's lawyer, a good-looking young man in his twenties, had already joined him.

"I want to go in there alone," Maya said to Marco.

"With how much it took just to arrest him?" Marco didn't look happy about it. "What if something upsets him in there? What if he gets aggressive?"

"Then you'll get in there quickly enough," Maya said. "But I don't want to risk him seeing us as pressuring him too much. He might refuse to say anything then. I think we have to take this gently."

"There's a gentle way of asking if he's a murderer?"

If there was, then Maya was determined to find it. She took a breath, forced herself to smile, and walked in.

Tommy's lawyer got the first words in. "I am not happy with the way my client has been treated. Tommy does not do well with stressful situations, and being violently restrained definitely counts as stressful."

Tommy. So this was a lawyer who knew him well. Possibly even a friend.

"Unfortunately, it was necessary to ensure that no one else was hurt. How are you feeling now, Tommy?" Maya asked.

She saw Tommy pause, as if trying to work out exactly how he *did* feel.

"My eye aches. Those people hit me. They're meant to be arbiters. They're meant to be neutral."

Meaning what? That they were meant to stand back while Tommy attacked one of their number? Maya didn't say that, though. She didn't want to turn this into a confrontation if she could avoid it.

"You did hit one of them, Tommy," Maya pointed out.

"She wouldn't let me finish," Tommy said, as if it were the most obvious thing in the world. "They all want to see me make puzzles, but then they won't let me finish them." He seemed to think for another moment or two. "I'm sorry I hit her, obviously."

"Are you?" Maya asked. "Or is that just something you know you ought to say?"

He shrugged then.

"Listen, Detective…," Tommy's lawyer began.

"Agent," Maya corrected him. "Agent Maya Grey, with the FBI cold cases unit."

The lawyer didn't look impressed. "So now the FBI is called in because of a scuffle at a competition? This isn't even a matter in which the FBI has jurisdiction."

"I'm in town on a different matter, which I believe might have connections to the world of puzzle solving," Maya said. "I was at the event because of that, so I happened to see your client strike one of the arbiters."

"That," the lawyer said, "is not Tommy's fault."

Maya looked at him levelly. "Explain."

"Tommy, as you have probably seen, is a savant when it comes to puzzles. He's also on the autistic spectrum. He is disturbed when people make it impossible for him to finish his puzzles, and that can lead to him… acting out."

Acting out seemed like a particularly polite euphemism for violently attacking people.

"I'm right here," Tommy said. "People talk about me like I'm not there all the time. Like I'm stupid. I'm not. My IQ is significantly above average."

"No one's calling you stupid, Tommy," Maya said. "I've seen your videos. What you do in them is impressive."

That got another shrug from Tommy. "It's *easy*. It's not my fault if other people can't do it."

"Of course," Maya said. "I've seen the other videos too. The one where you hit a man from behind with a chair? That wasn't just acting out. What happened there, Tommy?"

Tommy looked over to his lawyer, who gave a small nod.

"He threatened me. I couldn't let him threaten me. I had to do something. But I went too far. They put me on medication."

"Tommy has been on medication to curb the more… intense mood swings he's suffered for some time," his lawyer said.

"And how well has that worked?" Maya asked.

The lawyer paused, looking her over. He seemed to be trying to work out what Maya was trying to do there.

"Tommy pointed out before that he is highly intelligent. As am I, so please don't insult either of our intelligence by acting as if this is all some friendly chat. What do you want, Agent Grey? What is this actually about?"

Maya considered the best way to put it.

"There are two women, Trinity Dee and Christine Weller. I need to know if you had any connection with them."

She knew as soon as she said it that both Tommy and his lawyer understood the importance of it. The lawyer leaned forward as if he might stop Tommy from saying anything, but the puzzle champion was quicker.

"Had?" Tommy said.

"They were murdered," Maya said. "I'm here investigating Christine's death, and I believe Trinity's may be connected. Both of them were found with puzzle pieces on them, so I thought there might be some connection to the puzzling world."

She heard the lawyer cough pointedly, leaning over and looking worried. "I think you actually thought, 'here's someone who does puzzles and has been arrested for violence, maybe I can say it's him.' Is that closer to what you thought, Agent?"

"*Was* it you, Tommy?" Maya asked, not wanting to give the lawyer a chance to stop all of this before she could get answers.

"I've never met them," Tommy said.

"You're sure?" Maya asked.

"I remember things." Tommy closed his eyes. "When were they killed?"

"Christine died on the 23rd of April. Trinity was killed on the 13th of December, last year."

He nodded, seemingly to himself. "I was in Las Vegas from the 11th to the 15th of December. There was a convention."

"Tommy was the main attraction," his lawyer said. "So if that's all…"

Maya felt a flash of disappointment as she realized that this couldn't be the killer. Of course the answer wouldn't just drop into her lap like that. Still, she hadn't gone to the competition in the hope that she would find the killer there. She'd gone there hoping that she could get some help in identifying the puzzle pieces she'd found. She suspected that she had exactly the expert she needed sitting in front of her.

"Not quite," Maya said. "I believe that you couldn't have been the killer, Tommy, but my guess is that you know more about puzzles than anyone I've met so far."

"Yes," Tommy said. Apparently, he didn't feel the need for modesty.

"If you'd seen a puzzle piece, would you remember it?"

"Yes. I memorize them. It makes completing them faster."

His lawyer cut in then. "Is my client a suspect or a witness at this point?"

Maya gave him an even look. "He's not the killer I'm looking for, but he did just slap someone right in front of me. This is probably a good moment for him to be helpful, don't you think?"

She saw the lawyer bite his lip, then nod.

"Tommy, tell her what she wants to know."

Maya called up the pictures of the pieces that she'd taken on her phone.

"Do you recognize either of these pieces?"

Tommy took her phone from her staring at them almost with a kind of hunger, certainly with an intensity of concentration that was almost frightening.

"I haven't done a puzzle with these pieces," he said. "I would remember."

Maya felt the disappointment flooding through her, but struggled to push it down.

"Can you tell me *anything* about them?"

Tommy nodded. "They're from one of Hastel's patterns. H217. There are a couple of others that people think are the same, but you see the way the edges round here?"

Maya couldn't see it, but she guessed that if anyone would know, it would be him.

"I think they're both from the same puzzle," he said. "You see the way the tones of the colors are the same?"

"But the puzzle isn't one you've seen?" Maya insisted.

"I said that."

Actually, he'd said that he hadn't done the puzzle, but Maya guessed that he wouldn't have been able to see a puzzle without wanting to finish it.

"So it's… what? A custom job?"

Tommy nodded again. "Hastel does them, but some other people copy the patterns for one off designs. Some competitions order them, to try and stop people preparing. It slows me down, but it slows other people down more."

So, a custom ordered puzzle, probably from Hastel. Maya bit back her disappointment again. If Tony from Hastel hadn't been able to give them the details of someone who might have ordered it, then it seemed that there was no chance of finding the killer based on just the design.

Maya needed to think of something else, and now, she was running out of time.

CHAPTER TWENTY ONE

Yasmine was pretty much exhausted by the time she pulled up in her garage from work. Who would have thought that a day spent trying to extol the virtues of a new line of games would be so difficult?

That was marketing, though. Some days, all that would happen would be a meeting, and the whole thing would be counted as a great success. Other days, she would spend hours coming up with good copy only for it all to count for nothing, as a client or one of the partners rejected it.

Today had been the second kind of day. She'd spent the morning trying to reassure clients, because the kinds of people who worked in independent boardgame startups turned out to be all too aware of all the ways their new creations could fail. She'd gone out to lunch with one of Hastel's distributors, trying to persuade him to pick up a couple of lines. Then she'd run into Adam on the way back, and while he was always fun, he was also kind of exhausting.

Add to that a full docket of social media posts, ads, and press releases to write, and was it any wonder that she wanted to just slump back against the headrest of her Prius rather than even make the effort to get into the house?

Her phone buzzed, announcing a text from her colleague Allison.

A few of us are going to that boardgame café on Checkers Avenue. Do you want to join us?

Yasmine almost laughed at that. After a day of working with games people, did she want to go out and play more games? When Yasmine had come to Hastel, it had sounded like a dream job. A marketing firm that mostly dealt with small games companies in a kooky little town where boardgames seemed to be everything? It sounded a lot better than trying to dream up something new to say about life insurance or teeth whitening products.

The trouble was that *everything* here was boardgames. Yasmine didn't mind playing one from time to time, but here, it was an obsession. She didn't want boardgames all day at work, then every evening in her private life. Even the last guy she'd dated had been so caught up with them, he'd barely been able to talk about anything else. He'd had great abs and a better smile, but she'd only been able to put up with him for a month before she broke things off.

Not tonight, still have some work to do at home.

It was the kind of polite lie that kept a friendship going. Yasmine got out of the car and headed out to her mailbox, checking to see if there was anything there that she needed to read. Yasmine guessed that she of all people didn't get to complain about junk mail, but she still found herself quickly separating the contents, putting all the menus and the leaflets to one side so that she could throw them in the trash.

There was a blank envelope in there. Yasmin took it out and ripped it open. It was probably going to be some kind of marketing thing, but every so often a potential client just dropped something in her mail by hand. They thought that the best way to get taken on was to impress her with their commitment, and how amazing their game was.

Sometimes it even worked. Yasmine had picked up a couple of clients that way, and they'd done well, because it was good to see that a client was prepared to do what it took to break their product in the market.

So she opened the envelope and looked deep inside. Then she frowned, because the contents didn't make any kind of sense. A single puzzle piece sat in it, nestled there with nothing else beside it. No note to explain it, no additional information, not even a contact number.

Yasmine took out the piece, holding it up. It showed a red door, but nothing more than that. There was nothing on it that could identify it, nothing that could tell her more.

It was a teaser, obviously. It was the kind of marketing tactic that could work well when used properly. Yasmine should know, because she'd done it before, plenty of times. Done at the right time, it got people talking, wondering what was happening. It caught their attention, so that there was a market ready and waiting when she finally revealed what was happening.

Maybe everyone on the street got one of these pieces. Maybe this was all a part of someone else's marketing push. For now, though, Yasmine was far too tired to be interested. If this was someone trying to get her to represent them, they could get in contact normally, actually *telling* her about their game. Frankly, after something like this, even if they did get in contact, she might think twice about it.

Putting the puzzle piece back in its envelope, she tossed it in the trash.

Yasmine went back to the house, going in through the garage because she still had to lock up her car. She pushed the button on the remote that closed the garage door, then locked up her car as the door started to close. She headed for her house, taking out her keys and reaching for the door.

Yasmine heard a sound behind her then. The scuff of a boot on the driveway, the crunch of a step.

She started to turn, clutching her keys like a weapon, the way she'd heard that she was meant to. Although it occurred to her in that moment that she'd never actually used those keys against anyone when she was practicing, and that no one at the class she'd taken had actually been attacking her. In that moment, she felt something dropping around her throat, pulling painfully tight as a strong form pulled her back.

Yasmine flailed, her keys dropping from her grasp, forgotten now as she tried to breathe. She found herself dragged from her feet, panicking as she found that she couldn't breathe.

She wanted to fight back, but in that moment, she couldn't remember how. The pressure around her throat was immense.

"You know what you did!" a male voice snarled behind her. "It's time for you to pay!"

Yasmine wanted to cry out for help, wanted to find some way to make her attacker let go, but the pressure was starting to build up inside her head, and the edges of her vision were starting to fade into blackness.

She wanted to cry out that she didn't know what this was about, but it was already far, far too late.

CHAPTER TWENTY TWO

Maya sat in the office she shared with Marco with her head in her hands, trying to think. The two puzzle pieces sat on a desk in front of her, set there almost accusingly.

Maya stared at them as if she could get anything from them when the best puzzler in the town, probably in the country, had just told her that even he couldn't lead her to one specific person.

"Tony, it's Detective Spinelli," Marco said, making a call that Maya knew had to be made. "It's about the puzzle pieces we brought to you before. We're almost certain that they're custom made to your H217 pattern. Is there *any* way to trace a custom job like that?"

There was a pause as the line manager at Hastel's answered. One look at Marco's expression told her everything she needed to know.

"No, I understand." Marco shook his head. "Apparently, they don't keep pictures after the pieces are custom made. Part of what makes it attractive to people is that they know no one else is going to come along and order something exactly the same."

"And they have never had a reason to think that anyone would need to try to trace a particular pattern," Maya said, because why *would* anyone need to trace a pattern to solve a crime?

Except that she did now, and she couldn't. The puzzle pieces were getting her nowhere. Tommy Briner had an alibi. No one seemed to have a reason to want to hurt the victims, certainly not both of them.

Getting out her computer, Maya started to run searches on the two victims, trying to find any point at which the lives of Trinity Dee and Christine Weller intersected. She looked at the little that remained of their social media, at their jobs, at their hobbies.

There was nothing; no connection between the two except, presumably, in the mind of the killer. Maybe the fact that they looked so similar was enough for him. Maybe it was simply that he had a type, and everything else was just window dressing, designed to confuse things?

No, it couldn't be that. There had to be some way into this, or why would the Moonlight Killer have sent her here?

Maya groaned at that thought, pinching the bridge of her nose as she tried to stave off the headache that was threatening to blossom behind her eyes.

"It's ok," Marco said.

Maya shook her head. "It's really not."

"You'll think of something; you always do."

He was obviously trying to make her feel better, but right then, Maya wasn't sure if she *could* feel better.

"I'm not some kind of miracle worker, Marco. I can't pull answers out of thin air."

"It sometimes feels like you can," Marco said, moving to sit beside her.

Maya could feel how close he was there, feel the warmth of him. There were moments when she wished that he were closer still. There was something comforting about having him there like that, although it wasn't just comfort that Maya thought of when she looked at him, not even close.

If the moment had been different, Maya might have done something then, but it was impossible to give herself over to thoughts of how attractive the detective beside her was when the puzzle pieces were still sitting there in front of her. When she was slowly running out of time in which to solve this. When her sister was in danger, and she had to find a way to save her.

"Not now," Maya said, shaking her head. "I can't think of anything now."

Marco put a hand on her shoulder. "Maya, I've seen you do this before. Sometimes, you need to be reminded to take a breath."

"Is that what you think you're here for?" Maya demanded, and the words came out with more anger than she intended. "Are you here because you want to be, or just because you're worried about what will happen if you're not?"

"I'm not going to deny that I'm worried about you, Maya," Marco said. "You've already been pulled into another raid you didn't want to go on. I can see you obsessing about your sister-"

That was another thing he shouldn't have said. Maya found herself reacting without thinking.

"I don't need a babysitter. If that's what you've come to do, you might as well be in Cleveland. You have a job to do there."

It wasn't just anger at Marco, it was frustration at this whole situation, at being stuck. At the unfairness of it all, and at her own stupidity in expecting the Moonlight Killer to be fair about any of this. *Why* did he have to send her after something that couldn't be solved?

"I took a leave of absence from my job," Marco said, and his tone was slightly heated now too. "I came here because I care."

"Because you care, or because you don't believe that I can handle things on my own?" Maya shot back.

The problem with that was that *Maya* wasn't sure right then if she could handle things. She wasn't hearing Marco right then so much as her own doubts, but it didn't matter. She'd already said it, and she wasn't going to take it back.

She really didn't want to hear the answer, though.

Because of that, she was more than grateful when Detective Simms walked into the office, with a serious look on his face. Marco looked almost as grateful as she felt for the interruption.

"What is it, Detective?" Maya asked.

The detective looked a little flustered. "There's been a murder. A woman in her thirties. Dark hair. Found strangled just as she was going into her home."

Maya understood the importance of that at once. There was no way this wasn't connected to the other killings. She could argue with Marco later. For now, she had to get to the crime scene.

*

The house was one of a row of comfortable looking family homes that were almost identical. Or would have been, if this one hadn't been marked out by police tape and the flashing lights of squad cars.

Maya didn't see a lot of live crime scenes in her job. She came into things months, sometimes years, afterwards. She didn't get to see the moments when everything was abuzz with efforts to catch a killer, police canvassing the area looking for anyone who might have caught the least glimpse of something happening.

The house itself looked unremarkable. The garden had the well-kept but bland look that suggested the owner paid to have it looked after. The drapes visible through the window were a flash of bright yellow against the white exterior, but mostly, the place looked almost completely lacking in personal character from the outside.

Maya pulled up and she and Marco approached the crime scene without saying anything to one another. After what had just happened back at the station, Maya really didn't feel like saying anything to Marco at the moment.

He really felt that she needed someone to keep an eye on her so much that he'd taken a leave of absence from his job? Why would anyone do something like that? Maya had shown that she could look after herself plenty of times. She didn't need a detective following her around, second guessing her or the ways she did things.

Maya tried to ignore those thoughts, joining Detective Simms as he stepped from his own car, leading Maya and Marco towards the crime scene.

"What's the FBI doing here?" a uniformed officer keeping people back behind the crime scene tape asked.

Maya wasn't in the kind of mood to be argued with right then. "I'm here because I'm pretty sure this murder is linked to two more in this town. If there's going to be an argument over jurisdiction, it will be between my boss and yours, not between me and a beat cop."

The cop looked as if he might argue, but Detective Simms chose that moment to intervene.

"Let them through, Evans. They're here to help."

The uniformed cop lifted the crime scene tape, but didn't look happy about it. Maya walked past, to the spot where the garage stood open, revealing a forensics team working around the body of a woman. She lay there near a green Toyota Prius, just a stride or two away from the door that might have seen her safe.

One look at her features, and Maya knew that the cases had to be connected. It wasn't just that she was a little similar to Trinity Dee or Christine Weller: the three of them could have been sisters. Especially with her lying there like this, it was almost impossible to tell her apart from either of the others.

"We think she was ambushed as she returned home," Simms said. "The killer was waiting in her garage."

"More likely, he waited until she opened it and then crept in after her," Marco suggested.

"Why that way around?"

Maya answered. "There are no signs of damage to the garage doors to indicate a forced entry. Besides, it's a simpler way for them to have done this. And it's consistent with the way Christine Weller was killed.

A killer waiting, following, and then attacking right as she reached her door."

Around Maya, the forensics team were working with the kind of thoroughness that only this kind of crime had the budget for. They were sweeping every available surface for fingerprints or DNA. Maya could already guess at the problem with that, though.

"How many people have been through this garage so far?" Maya asked.

One of the forensics people looked up, shaking her head. "Too many. The neighbors saw her, so of course they ran in, and we also have everyone else who's been here in the last couple of months leaving traces."

And even if they found anything, it relied on the perpetrator already being in the police systems for it to be enough to identify him. The forensics might help with evidence when this came to a trial, but they weren't going to hand Maya an answer.

"What do we know about the victim?" she asked Simms.

"Her name is Yasmine Derry. She worked as a marketing consultant for a local firm."

"Does she have any obvious connection to Trinity Dee or Christine Weller?" Maya asked. If there was something clear, then it might point to a context in which the killer knew all three of them, and might make it possible to find him quickly.

The detective shook his head, though, which left Maya with the possibility that the killer was only selecting his victims because of the way they looked. If that was the case, then it might be that there was no trail leading back to him in their lives at all.

"What about the puzzle piece?" Maya asked the forensic team. "Have you found it yet?"

"What puzzle piece?" the forensic investigator who'd spoken before said.

"This killer leaves pieces from a jigsaw puzzle with the body," Maya explained. "With Christine Weller, it was in her bag. With Trinity Dee, it was tucked into her sock."

"We haven't found anything like that here."

Maya didn't know what to make of that. With both of the other murders, the pieces had been there, even if they'd been hard to find. They'd been the main factor that had led her to conclude that this was a serial killer, and not a pair of unconnected killings. Now, it seemed impossible that Yasmine Derry hadn’t been murdered by the same killer, but if that was the case, where was the jigsaw piece?

Was this all some kind of coincidence? Was this murder not connected at all? If Yasmine had looked even a fraction different, Maya might have believed that, but as it was, how could she? This had to be the work of the killer she was tracking, which meant that the jigsaw piece had to be here somewhere.

Maya just had to find it.

CHAPTER TWENTY THREE

Frank sat at the wheel of his van and waited, watching his target, determined that this time, everything would happen exactly the way he'd planned.

After the way things had gone wrong on the street, Frank had decided that taking Tori Blauer there like that represented too much risk. He'd found a new approach instead, a new opportunity.

Or at least, something that could be manufactured into an opportunity. That was what people got wrong, so often. They thought that chances simply happened, rather than being the natural consequence of careful preparation.

Take the art gallery that he was currently parked behind. Without preparation, that would have meant that he and his van were in full view of the cameras the gallery used to protect against theft.

Frank had dealt with those, though, hacking in and making sure they didn't record. He'd created his own blind spot for this.

That was stage one. Stage two was making sure that Tori Blauer would be here. Again, that had been simple enough to arrange. A couple of postcards, a couple of calls, and suddenly, this gallery wanted to exhibit her work.

A good hunter knew exactly what bait his prey required.

Now, he watched her approaching the rear of the gallery. The front was closed at this hour, so of course she would have to come around back. It helped that there was no one in there. Frank had arranged that too, with just a couple of messages to Tori purporting to be from the gallery owner's number. One to ask her to come a little early for their meeting, and then another, just a couple of minutes ago, as she arrived.

Come around back. We're bringing in pieces there.

Frank got out of his truck. He'd been careful with his disguise today: simple coveralls, enough changes to his features that he would be unrecognizable, a hat pulled down low over his face with the words *Arctus Conservation and Delivery* printed on it.

He wore dark glasses too. People saw what they wanted to see, but he wasn't going to give Tori Blauer any chance of seeing through to his real face. He'd already lost *one* bunny that way, after all.

Frank went around to the rear of his van, opening it and starting to unload paintings as Tori approached. Quick works by his own hand, with bunnies, of course. Enough to sell the illusion as his target got closer.

She looked excited, there in her dark skirt, formal blouse and jacket. She was obviously trying to look as professional as possible, obviously trying to make a good impression. She had three canvasses under one of her arms, and a bag that probably contained more work.

Frank wondered how horrified she would be once she realized just who she had made an impression on with her life.

Frank let her get closer.

"Excuse me," she said. "I'm looking for the gallery owner. Have you seen him?"

"Yes, hold on," Frank said. "I'll take you to him. I just have to get this…"

He stepped into the van, then knocked over the large statue he'd brought especially for this moment. Frank placed himself beneath it carefully, judging his angle so that it would appear that the full weight of the thing was on him, when in fact he was perfectly free.

He gave a cry of pain that would have impressed any Hollywood actor. But then, he'd heard plenty of such cries.

"Are you all right?" Tori asked, coming around to the back of the van. Frank saw her look of horror there. "Oh my God. What happened?"

"Get it off me!" Frank cried out as he lay there, trying to inject the right combination of pain, fear, and helplessness into the words. He'd come up with this scenario based on his potential bunny's reactions to the world around her: she cared too much, and tended to act without thinking through the consequences.

In that small respect, she reminded Frank of dear Maya.

She rushed forward, trying to help, getting close enough to reach out and touch.

That was when Frank removed a syringe from his coveralls, jabbing it into her and depressing the plunger.

"What are you doing?" Tori demanded, her expression suddenly frantic as she started to realize what was going on.

She turned as if she might run, but Frank was already out from under the statue. He grabbed her, holding her in place as she struggled to get free. She tried to hit out at him, but Frank had anticipated that, stopping the blows from landing. She reached for something that she could use as a weapon, but Frank caught her wrists, stopping that as well.

He got a hand across her mouth, stopping her from screaming. That was a bigger threat than anything she could do to him physically. That was the thing that could turn a controlled environment into something uncontrolled, far too quickly.

So Frank held onto her, ignoring the attempt that she made to bite him, feeling the attempts to thrash and escape start to slow. It was a feeling that he was familiar with, with a body fighting, then slowly coming to a halt as it ran out of strength. Usually, Frank savored it, feeling those fading moments as something truly intimate, truly connected.

Of course, in *thosc* moments, he had a ropc around somconc's throat. *That* was intimate in a way that no one else could understand, something between the two of them, something that, when they finally went still, only he would possess. This was a facsimile of that at best, but it still felt closer than anything Frank experienced with people in any other way.

Finally, Tori Blauer went limp. She feigned it at first, but Frank knew the difference. He knew the moment of unconsciousness, knew the moment of death. He could feel it. When she finally fell into true sleep, Frank laid her down as gently as he could.

He used tape to bind, gag and blindfold her, making sure that she would have no awareness of where she was going. He hopped down from the van, collecting his artwork, and hers, wanting to leave no trace behind.

Satisfied that he'd taken everything, Frank locked the doors of the van on his new bunny. It would be a long drive back, but it was worth it.

He had the number of bunnies he needed again now. He could do everything that was required. He had enough to make Maya follow this game through to the end, and then…

…well, then he would show her just how intimate those final moments could be.

CHAPTER TWENTY FOUR

Maya wasn't prepared to believe that there couldn't be a puzzle piece. It made no sense. Everything else about this crime said that it was by the same killer, so there *had* to be a puzzle piece here somewhere.

She squatted down, looking under the victim's car, checking that it hadn't fallen there. The space beneath seemed to be empty. She hurried over to a row of shelves containing tools, hoses, and all the other useful things that might otherwise have cluttered up a garage. Maya started to sort through a toolbox, making sure that it wasn't hidden somewhere in there.

Still nothing.

"There's nothing here," Detective Simms said. "I had our people search the garage and the house for evidence. If there were anything here to find, they would have found it."

"But they *didn't* find it," Maya replied. "Meaning that the puzzle piece must still be here somewhere."

She turned to the forensic investigators. "Have you checked her pockets? Her clothing? Anywhere the killer could have tucked a piece away? He put one in Trinity Dee's sock, so check there."

"We already-"

"Check again," Maya insisted, before the woman could even get to the end of that sentence. "I need you to find the piece."

She had nothing at the moment, no leads, and no sense of how she was meant to get closer to the killer. If this was a serial killer picking victims only because of how they looked, then trying to find connections between the victims wouldn't help her.

"Agent Grey," Detective Simms said. "I really think that you should step back and allow our technicians to do their jobs."

"Right now, the most important thing they can do is to find that puzzle piece," Maya replied. It was the only thing that mattered here. "This is the work of a serial killer who is the subject of an FBI investigation."

She didn't like being the one who had to assert her jurisdiction. She normally didn't want that kind of conflict with the local cops, so she didn't like trying to push Detective Simms out of his own crime scene. Here and now, though, if he wasn't going to help hunt for the puzzle piece, then he was in the way.

"That has yet to be proven," Detective Simms shot back. "Until and unless you find that puzzle piece of yours, this is my crime scene."

That was the other downside to this: if Maya couldn't find the puzzle piece, then she couldn't prove the connection to the other cases she needed to stay at the crime scene and look for the puzzle piece. It was an impossible situation, and one that left Maya in a dangerous situation. If she didn't find answers, then her sister was in danger.

Maya headed for the house. It was unlocked now, because the police had let themselves inside to search for any trace of the killer. Maya followed their steps, into a house so tastefully decorated that she suspected that it had been done by professionals. There weren't any personal photographs, nothing that made this place more Yasmine's, but maybe that said something in itself. Maybe it said how caught up in her job Yasmine had been, or that she wasn't planning on this as some kind of permanent home.

Maya started to go through the drawers there, feeling slightly frantic now. She had to find the puzzle piece. It had to be here somewhere. She knew that her only hope of finding the killer lay in finding some significance in the puzzle, in finding enough pieces to be able to trace it back to someone, or work out what it meant to them.

It had to mean *something.*

It wasn't just a lingering sense that the Moonlight Killer wouldn't send her to try to solve a crime if there was no solution there to be found; it was also the simple fact that the things a serial killer did meant something, even if it was only to themselves. They kept to their routines. This one should have been no more able to stop himself from leaving a puzzle piece than he could stop himself from killing in the first place. The puzzle pieces meant something, and so it was vital that Maya found this one.

Marco was in the kitchen now, following in her wake. He still had a worried expression, but Maya had had enough of him worrying about her. If he wasn't going to help, then the least he could do was keep out of her way while she did the things that might actually find answers in all of this.

“Maya, how would the killer have put a puzzle piece in the house?” Marco asked. “The door was locked when the police got here.”

Maya ignored him. She didn’t want to listen to someone who was just trying to hold her back right then, and she didn’t want to keep going with the argument they’d been having back in the police station.

Maya kept looking instead, making her way through the house. She saw a small stack of boardgames in one corner of the living room, but it didn’t look as if they were there to be played. Instead, each one had a series of sticky notes attached to it, with what seemed to be sketches or word clusters. Maybe ideas for marketing each one?

For now, they didn’t seem relevant, however. What mattered was finding the puzzle piece.

Marco was there then, with his hand on Maya’s arm.

“Maya, stop, you’re getting obsessed with this.”

Maya whirled towards him, and that close to him, she might normally have been thinking about how good it might have been to move even closer. She might have been taking in the warmth of him or the masculine scent. Right then though, she mostly just wanted to hit him for daring to grab her like that.

The main thing that stopped her was the memory of Tommy Briner hitting the arbiter, back at the puzzle competition.

“I’m not obsessed,” Maya snapped at Marco. “I’m trying to do my job.”

“By focusing on one thing to the exclusion of everything else? You think this is what your sister wants.”

“I think you don’t get to use Megan against me, not after I let you in,” Maya said.

She could see from Marco’s expression that he realized that he’d gone too far.

“Maya, I’m sorry, I didn’t mean that.”

Maya ignored him again, though, pulling clear of his grasp and walking away.

She knew that she couldn’t just keep searching frantically. No doubt, Marco had gone after her as a gentler option before Detective Simms tried to have Maya removed from his crime scene. She needed to think, and think fast.

What if the killer didn’t always place the pieces on the bodies after death? What if he left them where the victims would find them? It would explain why the pieces weren’t in a consistent place. Maybe

Christine Weller had picked hers up and put it in her bag as an oddity in the seconds before her death. It made less sense that Trinity Dee might hide the piece in her sock, but maybe she'd had it in her hand and the killer had put it there when she'd died?

Maya needed to think like Yasmine if she was going to understand how all of this had happened. She'd come home, gotten out of her car, and then what? Had she gone straight to her door and been killed? Was there anything else she might have done first?

The answer to that came to Maya in a flash: she might have checked her mail. Maya had started checking her own almost constantly when she was at home, waiting for the arrival of one of the postcards that might signal that the Moonlight Killer had another mystery for her to solve. Yasmine might not have that kind of incentive, but it still made sense that she might check the moment she got home.

Maya went back out to the front of the house, going out through the garage and heading straight for the mail box. It was empty. If there had been anything waiting for Yasmine there, it was gone. Yet there was no sign of any mail near her body.

Almost magnetically, Maya found her eyes drawn over to the trash cans near the side of the house. She went to them, opened the first up…

There on top sat a puzzle piece.

"I've found it!" she called out, as much as a vindication of everything she'd just done as because she wanted anyone else's help. "I've found the puzzle piece."

Maya took it out carefully, dropping it into a plastic evidence bag. She stared at it. This one seemed to have an image of a red door, with the upper portion of the frame and the door clearly visible. The frame had intricate carvings around it, obviously hand worked.

Marco and Detective Simms were there beside Maya now, and she displayed the puzzle piece proudly, holding it out so that they could see that she had been right to keep going with her search.

She could see the embarrassment on their faces. Marco, in particular, looked as if he understood just how wrong he'd been trying to talk Maya out of looking.

"It's the same guy," Maya said to Detective Simms.

"All right, I'll grant you that," the detective said, "but what does one more puzzle piece tell you? You can't even tell what the picture is."

Couldn't she? One piece had a stream, another a section of log. This last one had a hand carved red door. Maybe they weren't enough to construct a full puzzle, but Maya was pretty sure that she could guess at the subject matter.

"I think it's a picture of a log cabin," she said. "Somewhere by a stream."

She saw Detective Simms blink a couple of times, apparently in shock. "That… makes sense. But it still doesn't tell us about the killer. It could just be a standard design that he liked the look of."

"*Not* a standard design, a custom one," Maya said. "Tommy Briner told us that. Which means that this image means something to the killer." She found herself thinking about the custom image of the red windmill. "I'm willing to bet that this is a photograph of a real place, probably somewhere near here."

"You think you're going to find a killer by looking for a cabin with a red door?" Detective Simms said.

"A red door with these carvings," Maya corrected him. A red door would be unusual enough, but the carvings would probably be unique to one place. "Now, we just have to find it."

"Working on it," Marco said, and to Maya's surprise, he had his phone out, staring down at the screen. As much as Maya didn't want to talk to him right then, she knew that she had to.

"What are you doing?"

"I'm using Google Earth to look for local cabins near streams," Marco explained. "Then street view, or just uploaded photographs, to check for any with a door that matches. It's a long shot, but maybe, just maybe, we'll find something."

It *did* sound like a longshot, but also like the best hope they had of finding an answer quickly. If not then they were going to have to drive around to every cabin in the area, checking their doors by hand.

Maya waited impatiently while Marco kept scrolling. At the same time, though, she was impressed that he'd thought to do this. She'd started to think of him as a liability, holding her back, yet here he was helping, finding a way that might actually let them locate the house they needed.

"Not that one… no, that has a red door, but no carvings and no stream… that one has a green door… there! Maya, I think I've found it!"

He turned his phone so that Maya could see it. Sure enough, there was a log cabin with a red door on it. Someone had even posted pictures of it online, so that it was possible to zoom in and see every detail of the carvings around the frame. Maya compared them to the puzzle piece in her hand, and from the first moment she looked, there was no doubt in her mind that it was the same place.

Was *this* where the killer was, or was it just a place that meant something to him? Either way, it seemed to Maya that the only way to find him was to go there.

If he was there, then Maya would stop him, before he had a chance to kill anyone else.

CHAPTER TWENTY FIVE

From the moment she saw the cabin, Maya knew that it was the right place. She could feel her excitement building as she held up the puzzle pieces, trying to fit each one to the scene in front of her, as Marco pulled the rental car up in front of it.

She could see the stream, babbling along gently in the background. The log-built walls of the cabin were exactly the same shade as the picture. And there was the door, deep red, with carvings around the edges, the patterns of the swirls and the animals within utterly unique.

"It's here, isn't it?" Marco said.

He'd been the one to find this place, and now it sounded as though he wanted confirmation that he'd done it right. That he'd helped to make a difference here. Maya still couldn't let go of the fact that he'd come here to keep an eye on her, but she could give him that much, at least.

"This looks like the place," Maya said.

Which meant that they had to be careful.

"Does that mean that there's a serial killer sitting in there waiting for us?" Marco asked.

"It's possible." The truth was that Maya didn't know. Would a serial killer give them his address, even in such a coded form? Maybe it was a way of trying to prove how superior he was to them.

Maybe this was just a place that meant something to him, and coming here would only give them another clue, move them another step along the path to catching him. Whatever it was, though, they had to approach carefully.

The cabin sat in a small clearing with a stream running to one side and a meadow laden with wild flowers beyond.

Maya made her way out of the car, heading for the front door to the cabin. She had one hand on the butt of her Glock, half-expecting that the killer might come charging out at them with a weapon in his hands.

She found herself scanning the terrain around her for cover. There was a pile of logs split for firewood that might provide some protection off to one side of the cabin, and the car might also work, if they got down behind the engine block. Aside from that, though, it was hard to ignore just how exposed she and Marco were as they made their way over to the cabin.

Maya paused at the door, holding the third puzzle piece up to it, wanting to make sure that the carvings were correct. Certain now, she balled her hand into a fist and knocked hard on the door.

Beside her, Maya could see that Marco also looked ready for trouble. He had his hand on his own gun, ready to draw it at the least sign of danger. He stood slightly off to the side of the door too, obviously remembering the time when a suspect in one of the previous murders had tried to shoot them both through the door to his apartment.

That memory made Maya edge to the side as well, moving off the line of any burst from a shotgun. She took out her ID, holding it ahead of herself in her left hand, while her right hand stayed ready on her weapon.

"I'm coming, hold on!" a man's voice called from inside the cabin. Maya braced for the moment when the door opened.

When it did so, it revealed a tall, broad-shouldered man of about fifty, with a thick dark beard peppered with gray. He wore jeans, boots and a plaid shirt, while his hands were thickly calloused. Maya was looking at his hands in particular, because she wanted to make sure that they weren't reaching for a weapon.

It was all too easy to imagine those hands drawing a cord tight around a woman's neck.

"Yes, what is it?" he asked.

"Agent Grey, FBI," Maya said. Her ID was still out so that he could read it. "Is this your property?"

"That's right. I'm Edward Graham. What's all this about?"

Because there was no obvious threat yet, she wanted to take this slow. Three puzzle pieces weren't enough to arrest someone without anything else. Maya needed more evidence, and for that, she needed to stay calm, in spite of the tension running through her.

"This property has come up in relation to an ongoing investigation," Maya said. "I'd like to ask you some questions to try to establish if there is a connection. May we come in?"

"Can this wait?" Edward asked. "My wife is due to be released from the hospital today, and I want to be there."

"We'll try to be quick," Maya told him. "But the investigation is into a series of murders. It really can't wait."

Maya saw him tense, but she couldn't tell if that was just at the mention of murder or because he'd realized that he was about to be caught. She braced herself for the possibility that he might suddenly reach for a weapon, and beside her, she could see Marco doing the same. If Edward started to reach somewhere they couldn't see, then Maya was sure that both she and Marco would have their weapons cleared in an instant, ready to fire.

Instead of reaching for a weapon, though, he stepped back.

"I guess you'd better come in then."

Maya followed him inside, and the moment she did, she had confirmation that this was connected to the murders somehow.

Every surface was crammed with puzzles. There were particularly beautiful ones completed and framed on the walls like paintings. There were half completed ones that looked as if they contained many thousands of pieces on just about every horizontal surface. Boxes for more of them caught Maya's eye, stacked up practically everywhere there was enough room.

"What is all this?" she asked.

"All what?" Edward asked, as if he genuinely didn't see it all. "Oh, you mean the puzzles? My wife and I have always been into them. We're actually puzzle trainers."

"What's a puzzle trainer?" Marco asked.

"People come to us who want to compete. Putting them together as fast as possible, you know?"

Maya nodded. "We've seen a competition, and met a few of the main competitors. People have trainers, though?"

She saw Edward nod. "It's like anything competitive. People want to do the best they can. They want to win. And to do that, they take coaching from people who have done it before, and who know all the tricks of how to do it better."

Before she'd come to Hastel, Maya might not have believed it. Now, though, it seemed obvious. She doubted that Tommy Briner had a trainer like Edward in his corner, but she guessed that some of his rivals might. She guessed that in a town like this, it was completely conceivable that someone might make their living teaching people the best strategies to solve puzzles, or showing them how to rise to the top in the competition scene.

"You must know a lot about puzzles," Maya said, as Edward led them through into what was probably a living room. There were still puzzles everywhere. There was also an electric bandsaw set up in one corner, and Maya could see that a half-finished puzzle was there.

"You make your own?" Maya asked.

Edward nodded. "One of the ways I supplement my coaching income is to offer custom puzzles to people who come through the town. Tourists sometimes come in, get an afternoon of training, then buy a custom puzzle of their partner or their pet as a souvenir."

He shrugged, suggesting to Maya that it wasn't the side of his business that he was proudest of. Still, it offered her a chance to ask a question that might provide answers about the puzzle pieces she'd found so far.

"Do you cut them at random, or do you use standard patterns?" Maya asked. Before she'd come to Hastel, Maya wouldn't have even known to ask the question.

"For some of them, I'll cut a custom pattern," Edward said. "But for all the competition stuff, I cut them to standard patterns. Pattern recognition is a big part of it. All the old Hastel patterns."

"H217?" Marco said, obviously getting what Maya was driving at.

"Well… yes, I guess so," Edward replied.

It might just be a coincidence, but put together with the jigsaw pieces Maya had, she was sure that it wasn't. She kept looking around the room, trying to find anything else that potentially connected to the case.

Then she saw it, and Maya froze in place as she stared. There was a completed puzzle on one wall, obviously custom made, clearly produced from a photograph.

It was of a woman in her thirties, with dark hair and piercing eyes. She was slender, and even though Maya had never seen the woman before, she felt as if she knew her. The details of her face were unfamiliar, but Maya had seen the general outline of her face before. She'd seen three faces that were almost identical to hers.

Christine Weller, Trinity Dee and Yasmine Derry could have been her sisters, yet somehow, Maya knew that this was more than that. This was the archetype, the original. *This* was what the killer was basing his choice of victim on. And since this picture was up there on that wall, it meant that she looked at Edward with renewed suspicion.

She couldn't look away from the picture now. Even so, she managed to force herself to ask the questions she needed to ask.

"Edward, where were you last night?"

It was the question that mattered most.

"Last night?" he asked, as if he couldn't quite take in the question.

"Last night," Maya said. "Where were you?"

"I was here," Edward said, as if it were obvious. As if there were nowhere else that he would be likely to be.

"All evening?" Maya asked. She needed to be clear about exactly where Edward Graham had been at the moment when Yasmine Derry had been killed.

"I was working on a couple of custom puzzles here," Edward said.

"Alone?" Maya asked.

She saw Edward nod. "My wife is in the hospital. I told you, I'm waiting for her to be released."

"What about on the 23rd of April?" Maya asked.

"I don't remember," Edward said. "Why would I remember that?"

There didn't seem to be any point in asking about the murder before that. If he couldn't remember where he'd been when Christine Weller had died, there was no chance that he would remember where he'd been when Trinity Dee had been killed.

Which meant that he had no alibi.

Maya started to put the pieces together, like one of the puzzles sitting around the room. The cabin that was pointed to by the puzzle pieces she'd found at the murder scenes. The connection to the world of puzzles. The fact that there was a picture of a woman who looked exactly like the victims sitting there on the wall. The complete lack of any alibi.

The conclusion seemed clear: she was standing across from a man who might be a serial killer.

"I think I need you to come down to the Hastel police department with us," Maya said. Everything so far was circumstantial, so she didn't want to arrest Edward outright, but she needed to bring him in and see if there was any kind of forensic tie to the scenes.

"I can't do that," Edward said. "I told you, my wife is being released from the hospital today. I have to be there for her when she comes out. I'm not leaving Delia stranded."

Maya could hear the concern there, but this was about murder.

"We'll send someone to collect your wife," she said. "But right now, we need you to come downtown."

"I really don't think-"

"Mr. Graham, this isn't optional," Maya said. "You can come with us voluntarily, or you can come with us in cuffs. It's your choice."

Maya put some steel in her voice, and she could see that it took Edward a little aback.

"I guess I'd better come with you, then."

Did Maya have the killer in her hands? She didn't know yet, but she would know soon.

CHAPTER TWENTY SIX

Maya sat across from Edward Graham in the interrogation room, in there alone with him, trying to see the serial killer in his expression, his body language, his eyes. She'd left Marco outside the interrogation room, wanting to do this alone.

The problem was that it was impossible to simply see the evil in someone. Maya needed evidence. She needed to find a way to get him to talk, letting slip something that would prove what he'd done.

"Why am I here?" Edward asked. "I have to go collect my wife from the hospital."

"We'll make sure that someone meets her," Maya assured him. Would a psychopath be worried about his wife like that? Was it just a way for him to deflect attention, or try to find a way out of this?

Then again, there were plenty of examples of killers who'd held down a normal family life, then gone out to murder people.

"She's just coming to the end of her treatment," Edward said. He hesitated then. "They're… sending her home so that we… so that we can spend some time together before she…"

Before she died. Under any other circumstances, Maya's first instinct would have been to let him go, to help him be with his wife, but right then, there were things that couldn't be let go.

"I still don't understand why you've brought me in," Edward said.

"Because three women have been murdered," Maya replied. "And there's a connection to you and your house."

She set the three puzzle pieces that had been left with the bodies on the table between them.

"This *is* a picture of your house that the puzzle is building, right?" Maya asked.

"Well… yes, I think so."

"These puzzle pieces were left on the bodies of three women, the most recent of them killed just last night."

Maya saw the surprise on his face at that. Was it genuine, or was he just a good actor?

"That's why you asked me where I was?" The importance of that seemed to sink in for the first time. "You think I killed someone?"

"There are three dead women," Maya said. "All of whom look *remarkably* like the puzzle portrait that is up on the wall of your cabin."

By now, of course, it would have been removed. Hastel PD were there, searching the house thoroughly for any evidence that might link him to the crimes.

"That's my wife, Delia," Edward said. "You think I want to hurt women who look the way she did twenty years ago?"

"I don't know," Maya said, looking at him levelly. "Do you?"

"No, of course not!" he replied, looking upset that Maya would even ask the question. "What kind of person do you think I am?"

"I think that you're someone who's obsessed with puzzles," Maya said. "I think that you live at the right house, you have a picture that looks almost identical to the victims, and you have no alibi for any of the murders. Would you like to explain any of that?"

"I just explained about my wife," Edward said. "And the puzzles… I told you at the house. My wife and I train people for puzzle competitions. I used to be a competitive puzzler, and then we realized that it was easier to run things more from the coaching side, teaching kids, or people who come in and want to learn, or just tourists who want to say they learned puzzling in the boardgame capital of America."

It sounded plausible, but it also did nothing to explain why the house was in the puzzle pictures, or the victims all looked the way they did. Maya got the feeling that if she just kept asking the same questions, though, she would only get the same answers from Edward Graham, whether they were the truth or carefully pre-prepared lies.

"I'll give you a minute or two to think," Maya said, standing. "You have to know how this all looks."

She left the interrogation room, giving Edward some time to consider his current position. Maybe it would be enough to persuade him to confess. Or, if it really wasn't him, maybe it would give him enough time to remember where he'd been on the days when Trinity Dee and Christine Weller were murdered.

Marco was waiting for her when Maya got outside.

"I looked up his record," Marco said. "There's some stuff from when he was teaching kids."

"When he was teaching?" Maya said, catching that part. "It's not something they currently do?"

Marco shook his head. "Maybe they teach a few adults here and there. Tourists, like he said. But with kids… I don't think they'd be allowed after this. No one managed to make any charges stick, but the files say a lot about abuse and neglect there at their house. Kids with unexplained bruising, stories about harsh training methods… this is not a good guy we're dealing with."

The news seemed at odds with how willing to cooperate Edward Graham was, and with his general demeanor, yet maybe that just showed how dangerous he was. Maybe it showed that he was an expert in hiding his real self from the world, regardless of what he did?

Detective Simms came up, and it seemed that Maya was back in his good graces again, given the smile he directed her way as he approached.

"You've done it," he said. "You've actually caught him. I always knew there was something weird about Edward Graham."

"You've run into him before?" Maya asked. The files were one thing, but hearing it from one of the local cops was quite another.

She saw Detective Simms shrug. "He used to be a big deal around Hastel. A town like this, if you're a major puzzle competitor, there's always a good chance people have heard of you."

Maya thought of Tommy Briner, the supposed rock star of puzzling, and how people reacted around him. It wasn't inconceivable that Edward had been the same, back in the day.

"So what happened?" Maya asked.

"If you've read his files, you know already," Detective Simms said, with a note of distaste. "People sent their kids to them to train, thinking it would be good for them to learn to do a few puzzles. Next thing, there are stories of abuse floating around. Kids who were traumatized by their methods. Kids who didn't want to talk about any of it. Honestly, if half of that shit had happened today, we'd have locked them up and thrown away the key."

"But it didn't happen then?" Maya asked.

"From what I hear, the department couldn't corroborate enough stories, couldn't get any physical evidence, and… well, you know what it was like back then, when it was just the word of a bunch of kids against grown adults." Detective Simms sounded pained by it, and also embarrassed. He obviously felt that his force should have done more at the time.

Maya understood. In cases where there was abuse and neglect, getting kids to speak out was often hard, but backing up what they said with additional evidence could be even harder. A lot of them felt as though they wouldn't be believed, for the simple reason that often, they weren't. Twenty years ago, it seemed that the police in Hastel hadn't felt as though they could prove enough, and Maya could only guess at the damage that failure might have done.

Was it so inconceivable that a man who had started off with that kind of abuse and neglect might move on to more?

"How is the search of his property going?" Maya asked. "Is there anything else to connect him to the murders?"

"We haven't found physical evidence," Detective Simms said. "My team completed its sweep and has come back. But that doesn't mean that we're going to stop. You have this guy here voluntarily so far? I want to arrest him and hold him."

"Maybe," Maya said.

"Maybe?"

"I want to leave it as long as possible before committing to that. He'll lawyer up, and we'll have nothing. If it looks as though he's going to leave, then yes, but not until then. Especially when we don't have physical proof."

Detective Simms looked over to Marco as if that would change things.

"Tell your partner that we have plenty. He'll crack."

"Maybe he will," Marco agreed, "but I've learned to trust Maya's judgement on this kind of thing."

"Unless we do get a confession, what do we have?" Maya asked. "A bunch of circumstantial evidence that doesn't connect him definitively to the crime. Unless you found the rest of the puzzle that the pieces came from?"

That would be the key piece of evidence if they could find it. If they could take that one off, custom puzzle into a courtroom and set the final pieces in place in front of a jury, that would almost certainly be enough to convince them. Without it, Maya wasn't so sure.

The killer would have that puzzle close, would *need* it close. So why wasn't it at the house?

They needed to come at all of this from another angle.

"Marco, can you take over the questioning here?" Maya asked.

"Sure," Marco said. "Maybe he'll even confess. You're going somewhere?"

Maya nodded. "He said his wife is being released from the hospital. She might be able to tell us something, provide us with the proof we need. So I'm going to make sure that I'm the one who picks her up when she leaves."

*

Driving to the hospital gave Maya plenty of time to think about the case. It felt as though she was close to an answer, with all the pieces there in front of her, just waiting to be fit together properly.

Yet, like Tommy Briner back at the competition, it still felt as if something was missing.

Maya could understand how badly the local cops wanted to put away Edward Graham. She could understand Marco wanting to take another run at him, too. Yet something still didn't feel quite right. Was it just the shock that Maya had seen on his face when she'd talked about the murders? He'd certainly looked as though he'd never heard anything about them before. Could that be faked?

And where was the puzzle?

That was the part that continued to eat at Maya. The puzzle should have been there. It was the key piece of evidence. The killer might hide it, but it would have to be close to him.

So much of the rest of it pointed to a connection to Edward and his wife, though. The puzzle pieces were definitely of his house, the puzzle of his wife on the wall resembled the victims so closely that it was uncanny. The reports of abuse suggested a pattern of violence that might have escalated.

Maya tried to make those pieces fit together. Was it possible that Edward Graham, a violent man with a history of abuse, had gone from hurting kids to killing women? Had he gone by way of hurting his wife. Was that the reason that she was in the hospital?

It was one possibility, but it still didn't sound quite right. Especially when they couldn't find the puzzle. Was there another explanation?

Maya turned the evidence over and over in her head, trying to look at other ways it might fit together. She found herself thinking about that picture on the wall, of Edward's wife.

A picture from twenty years ago, when the abuse had been taking place.

That thought seemed to bring everything into focus. Why would Edward target women who looked the way his wife had looked *then*? There was no reason for it. But someone who remembered her from that time, and who hated her?

Was *that* the answer to all of this?

Maya realized in that moment that Edward Graham wasn't the killer. He wasn't behind this, and nor was Delia Graham. They were at the heart of all this, but they weren't the ones doing this.

They were the targets.

Which meant that going to collect Delia Graham wasn't about getting to a witness anymore in order to find evidence of what her husband had done. It was about getting to her before a killer realized where she was and tried to finish what he'd started.

Maya hit the gas pedal, hoping that she would get to the hospital in time.

CHAPTER TWENTY SEVEN

Samuel was coming for her now. Finally, after all this time, and everything she'd done, he was going to make sure that Delia Graham got what she deserved. There were so many emotions running wild in him as he walked into Hastel's hospital that he had to force himself to be still, to not let any of it show on his face.

He'd had a lot of practice at that, thanks to her.

Samuel had been eight when his parents had started taking him to the Grahams's cabin for puzzle lessons. Eight years old when the abuse had begun. Eight years old when a grown woman had started to tear his life apart.

His hands curled into fists as he thought of it, but he forced himself to keep walking into the hospital. He could make himself do anything he needed to now. He was strong.

She had seen to that. His parents had thought that learning to concentrate on the puzzles might help with his ADD. They'd seen that he liked playing with them, so they thought it was the obvious thing to do. They'd given him over into the care of a monster, and called it doing the right thing.

Well, Samuel was going to do the right thing today. He was going to end this.

He walked up to the reception desk, forcing himself to smile, to be personable and charming, to fake all the things he didn't feel as he stood there in front of the young woman running the desk.

"Hi," he said. "I'm here to collect someone who is being released today."

"What's the name?" the receptionist asked.

"Delia Graham."

Somehow, he managed to say that name without a hint of the hatred that he felt.

She'd made him so good at hiding his emotions, his thoughts, his feelings, that sometimes even he didn't know what they were anymore. Her idea of a puzzle "lesson" had been to make Samuel sit there, doing the same puzzle, over and over. Every time he spoke or fidgeted, she hit him, always where it wouldn't show. If he cried from it, she hit him harder. If he messed up the puzzle…

Samuel's hands twitched reflexively at the thought of the hard wooden cane being brought down across them.

"Is everything all right?" the receptionist asked.

"Everything's fine," Samuel told her. The phrase that had been beaten into him. The one that he'd been told to say when anyone asked, because he wouldn't be believed, because she would just hurt him worse. "I'm just a little worried about Delia. I'm a family friend."

The receptionist tapped in a couple of things at her computer.

"It says here that her husband is the one who is due to collect her."

"He's been delayed," Samuel said. "The police have asked him to help them with something, and obviously Delia still needs a ride home."

When he'd heard about that, and Hastel's puzzle community was such a small place that it was impossible *not* to hear about that, he'd been delighted. Edward might not have hurt Samuel the way that *she* did, but he hadn't done anything to stop it, either. Samuel had seen his opportunity, and now he was going to take it.

He was going to have revenge for all the pain she'd inflicted. Maybe then, the memories would stop. Maybe the puzzle would stop haunting his dreams.

"I'll have to check if that's ok," the receptionist said. "We can't just release patients to anyone."

"I understand," Samuel replied, although inside, there was the barest flutter of panic there. What if they wouldn't let her go with him? What if they tried to stop him?

In that case, he would leap forward and kill her right in the middle of the hospital's waiting area. He would end this, any way he had to.

The receptionist made a call. "Hi, I have someone here to collect Delia Graham. It's not her husband, though. Yes, I understand."

She turned to Samuel.

"I'll need to see some kind of ID."

Samuel had a fake driver's license, specifically for moments like this. He'd been careful about all of this. He handed it over, waited for the receptionist to look at it, and then saw her nod.

"That's great, thank you," she said. "We'll get Delia down, and if she wants to go with you, then that's fine."

If she wanted to go with him? That was the hard part of this. Maybe she would take one look at him, see the boy she'd abused all those years ago, and call for help. Maybe she would understand what was happening and try to run.

If she did, Samuel would kill her, there in the open.

He waited, sitting there on one of the hard plastic chairs in the waiting area for her to arrive. He sat perfectly still, because he'd learned to do that. He'd learned that moving only led to pain. She'd taught him that lesson.

The puzzle swam in his mind's eye while Samuel waited, the pieces going together one after another, always the same order, always the same picture. The cabin, built again and again in his head, just as he'd built it again and again under Delia's direction.

"But why can't I do a different *puzzle?"* his young voice asked in his memory.

She'd struck him then.

"You need to learn to focus, you little brat. Start again, from the beginning."

He'd thought that he was over it. He'd thought that he'd survived and come through it. The lessons had ended. Then, eight months ago, he'd seen her. Only it hadn't been her, Samuel knew now. It had just been a woman who looked so much like her that it was uncanny.

In that moment, all the pain had come rushing back to him. It had been as though he'd been there again, forced to complete the same puzzle over, and over, and over…

He'd had to kill her. He'd had to make it stop. There had been no other way.

He still had the puzzle. His parents had bought it for him at the end of his lessons, like it was some kind of mark of achievement. Or more likely, Delia had told them that it was his favorite, and that completing it calmed him. He kept it in a box, where he couldn't see it, but even then, he knew that it was there.

That was why he'd left a piece with the body. So that he would never have to complete the puzzle again.

"She'll be down in a moment," the receptionist called over to Samuel.

He remembered to smile back, to fake the kind of feelings that other people seemed to find so easy. He hadn't found them easy ever since they'd taken him to the cabin. He'd had to learn how to pretend, just so that he could fit in. Even then, it was hard. People looked at him and it was as if they could sense some of the ball of pain knotted up inside him.

Then *she* entered the waiting area, and it was all Samuel could do not to throw himself forward to attack her there and then.

Delia was leaning on the arm of a large orderly. She looked older now, although the same sharp features were still visible under graying hair. She looked gaunt, as if the illness that had brought her here had taken away a lot of the strength she'd had. She seemed smaller now, although that was simply because Samuel wasn't a child anymore. He wasn't small enough for her to hurt, now.

Quite the opposite.

When he'd seen women who looked like her, he hadn't been able to stop himself. A part of him had still been a small child, trapped in the process of making her puzzle again and again. A part of him had been caught up in his anger so much that he'd genuinely believed that they were her.

Yet here was the original, right in front of him. It was almost done.

Samuel moved forward, making himself smile.

"Delia, there you are. I'm afraid Edward can't come to bring you home, so he asked me if I would mind doing it."

"Edward?" her voice came out with an edge of fuzziness to it. "Edward sent you?"

The orderly with her spoke then. "Delia here is on a lot of pain meds. Well, you know how her condition is. It means she'll be a little out of it for a while."

"That's all right," Samuel said. Just as long as there was enough of her left to understand what she'd done before the end came. With the others, he'd killed them quickly, just so that their faces couldn't haunt him, but with her, he wanted to take his time. He wanted her to feel some fraction of the pain she'd inflicted before she died. "I'm sure it will be ok."

"Just to check," the receptionist said to Delia. "You do know this man?"

She gave Samuel an apologetic smile, like it was all just routine, but he felt anxiety rising inside him. If Delia said no, he would have to do this now, in front of them all. And if they tried to stop him…

He would go through them.

Samuel could feel Delia's eyes roving over him, obviously looking for some sign that she knew him.

Samuel found himself wondering if she would recognize him. Would she look at him and see the eight-year-old boy she'd hurt so much, the one she'd tortured while claiming that it was for his own good? Would she see him as he had been, the way he saw the younger version of her every time that he looked at her?

"I…" It seemed to be hard for her to focus. She managed something that might have been a nod.

Did she recognize him, or was she just jumping at the chance to get out of there? Samuel didn't care which it was right then. All that mattered was that the receptionist pushed over a couple of release forms for Delia to sign. Samuel pressed a pen into her hand, helping to steady her arm while she did it.

The orderly and the receptionist looked over at him with something like approval for being so helpful. Samuel supported Delia as they started to move together towards the door.

"Come on Delia," Samuel said. "Let's get you out of here."

And then to a nice, quiet place, where he could finally do what he had to do to make the puzzle leave his head.

"It's time to take you home."

CHAPTER TWENTY EIGHT

Maya wove through the traffic, wishing not for the first time that rental cars came with blue lights and sirens. She was speeding, but almost hoped that a traffic cop would pull her over so that she could pull her badge and insist on help getting to the hospital that much faster.

The more she thought about all of this, the more convinced she was that Delia Graham was in danger. With Edward in custody, and Delia due to be released from hospital, the killer had a clear shot at her. Maya felt almost certain now that he would take it.

Maya thought about calling in for help, but she didn't. Part of it was that she still wasn't certain about this. She needed to know for sure that something was happening before she called for backup. Another part of it was that Maya wasn't sure who she could trust right now. Even Marco was there to stop her from running off wildly after things like this.

Sometimes, it was better to work alone.

She skidded into the parking lot of the hospital, then ran for its entrance, hurrying through into a waiting room filled with people waiting for treatment. Maya flashed her badge at the receptionist.

"Delia Graham. Where is she?"

The receptionist only looked flustered for a moment or two before she recovered.

"Ms. Graham? Oh, she left about ten minutes ago."

"She left?"

It felt like the culmination of all Maya's fears. The thought of what might be happening to her even then sent a thread of terror through her.

"Yes, there was a young man who came to collect her. He said that her husband was helping the police with something, so he was there to be Ms. Graham's ride home."

"Home? You're sure?" Maya said.

The receptionist looked a little puzzled. "Where else would he take her?"

Maya was already running out to the car, trying to work out which direction the killer might have taken Delia in.

In theory, he could have taken her anywhere in the city. He could find any out of the way place and kill her. He could have already done it, and her body might be lying in an alley somewhere, waiting to be discovered.

Maya knew that she had to call it in, so she took out her phone and called Marco.

"Maya, is everything ok?"

"I just got to the hospital. Delia Graham has already been collected by a young man claiming to be a friend. I think the killer has her."

"That's… what do you need?"

At least he didn't waste any time arguing about it.

"I need you to talk to Simms, and get as many cops out looking as possible. The hospital will have camera footage of the killer as he left with her. I need them to cover as many locations they might have gone to as possible."

"And where are you going?" Marco asked.

"I'm going to check out a hunch."

She hung up, because it was better if Marco spent his time coordinating the search than chasing around after her. Maya could handle this part alone.

Her hunch was a simple one: that the killer hadn't been lying when he'd said that he was taking Delia home. That had been the place in the puzzle, after all. It was a place that meant something, just as Delia as herself twenty years ago meant something.

This was a boy who'd been abused there, by her. Maya was almost certain of it. The rest made sense when she looked at the killings like that. It explained why the killer might focus on just that one face, and on leaving that one puzzle. It explained why there was the connection to the Grahams.

And it meant that, if he wanted to finish this somewhere significant to him, the cabin was the only place that he would take Delia Graham.

*

Maya sped up the country roads beyond the city, taking them at a speed that she was certain wasn't safe. Trees flashed past outside her window, and Maya felt her rental car lurch as she threw it around a corner, but she didn't slow down. There was no *time* to slow down.

Even now, it was possible that she was too late. In the other killings, the murderer had struck quickly, when his victims had been right on their doorsteps. He'd killed them and moved away, before anyone could see him.

Somehow, though, Maya suspected that this murder would be different. This time, the killer actually had the woman who had tormented him, rather than someone who merely looked like her.

He wouldn't kill her quickly. This meant too much to him for that.

At least, she hoped so.

The cabin was ahead now, and Maya could see the strange car parked outside: a Citroen that hadn't been there when Maya had visited earlier. She looked around, half hoping for police cars, still there for the search, but Detective Simms had already told her that his team had moved on, finding nothing.

Maya was alone for this.

She got out of her car and approached with her weapon drawn, holding it two handed. Maya tried the door and found it was unlocked, pushing it open.

The cabin was empty.

Had Maya gone to the wrong place? Had she made a mistake even now? One that might get a woman killed?

Maya made her way through the house, clearing the rooms, one by one. The living room was empty. The same went for the kitchen and the bedroom. What was left? Maya stepped outside, trying to make sense of it. The strange car was still there in front of the house.

They *had* to be here somewhere.

That just left the outbuildings. Maya started to make her way around to them, gun still out, not wanting to take any chances.

She was walking past one of the bigger outbuildings when she thought she heard a noise from inside. Maya burst in, gun levelled, and what she saw there made her freeze in place for a second.

She saw Delia Graham there, seated at a table, with a puzzle set out in front of her. Maya recognized her instantly, thanks to both the puzzle portrait on the wall and the similarities she had to the three victims. She could have been their mother, with the same fine boned features and dark hair, only twenty years older than they were.

Maya recognized the puzzle, too. The picture was of this cabin, this place where so much had happened already. Delia was putting it together with shaking hands, a piece held trembling between her fingers.

She looked at Maya in shock and fear, then Maya saw her eyes dart to the side, looking at a spot behind Maya.

Maya reacted in time, throwing up a hand as the strangling rope came into her vision. She managed to get her hand between the cord and her neck, stopping it from cutting in and strangling her even as the killer behind her dragged her to the ground.

Maya tried to turn her gun on him, but at such close quarters the angle was wrong, and he managed to wrench it from her hand. The most Maya could do was knock it away so that the killer wouldn't end up with her weapon to use against her.

That just left the rope that he was still trying to drag tight around Maya's throat, hauling back on it with a strength born of fury.

"Why did you have to interfere?" he snarled at her, in a rough voice. "Why did you make me do this?"

Maya drove her elbow back at him, making a little space, then pummeled her arm to the far side of his body, using it to turn her to face him. He was young looking, tall, with dark hair and handsome, slight, soft features. He looked unremarkable, apart from the rage in his eyes. He was still trying to pull on the ligature, trying to drag it tight, but Maya kept her hand in the way, blocking it as he tried to garotte her.

She drove the fingers of her other hand into his throat, forcing him away from her, gagging. It gave Maya a chance to get up, trying to get to her gun, but the killer leapt after her. They were grappling now, and it was obvious that her opponent knew how to fight, because he avoided Maya's first attempt to throw him to the ground and came back with one of his own, tackling her and slamming her into the hard wood of the floor. He threw a punch that Maya managed to block, but then he was up, backing away from her.

He snatched up a poker from the fireplace, swinging the metal of it straight at Maya's head.

She managed to dodge the first blow, keeping moving, trying to think of a way to finish this.

"I know what this is about," Maya said. "I know you were abused here."

"You don't know anything," he snarled back. "You don't know what it was like to be made to sit at that table, completing the same puzzle over and over. To be hit if I moved, or I got anything wrong."

He swung at Maya again. This time, she wasn't quite fast enough, and the poker caught her a glancing blow across the side of the head. It wasn't enough to knock Maya out, but she felt the dizziness and disconnection that came after being hit hard. She knew she wouldn't be able to take too many more hits like that.

"And that's your excuse for killing three women?" Maya demanded. "They didn't do anything to you."

He circled her now, staying between Maya and her Glock so that she couldn't lunge for it.

"I looked at them, and I saw *her*. All of them were her. All of them were the images in my head, doing nothing but hurt."

If it had been any other circumstances, Maya might even have felt sorry for him. If he hadn't killed three women, she might have felt some sympathy, might even have helped make sure that Delia got the prison time she deserved. Now, though, she was facing a monster who had to be stopped.

"Why now?" Maya asked, as she dodged back from another blow. "You could have done this at any point."

He jabbed a finger in Delia's direction. "Because she's dying! I was getting on with my life. I was getting past it all. Then I saw an appeal online to help a 'beloved local figure'. It brought it all back I saw her everywhere. I saw the puzzle in my head. It wouldn't go away."

He thrust the poker at Maya, keeping her back.

Maya couldn't find a way past the poker, to take him down. She needed to think of something, because currently, the killer was the one with all the weapons, and Maya had nothing. Worse, he wasn't leaving any obvious openings, nothing that she could exploit.

An idea came to Maya, and she stepped over to the table, sweeping the puzzle to the floor. The puzzle pieces scattered across the cabin, and she saw the killer's eyes trying to track every one.

"No!" he cried out, and that was the moment when Maya lunged at him.

She got inside the sweep of the poker, managing to get a grip on it. She wrenched at it, kicking out at the killer even as she did so. She managed to wrench the poker out of his hands, but he threw it to one side even as she did it, so that it went clattering away.

He got a punch in then, catching Maya hard. She stumbled, managing to go get a punch of her own in, but then the killer tripped her and Maya went tumbling to the floor.

She hit the wooden floor hard, the breath going out of her body in a whoosh. Maya did her best to struggle back to her feet, but for a second, she didn't have enough air in her lungs to do it.

In that second, the killer had enough time to pick up Maya's Glock and level it at her.

"You shouldn't have tried to stop me," he said. "You shouldn't have gotten in my way."

In that moment, Maya knew that she was going to die. There was no cover to duck behind, no time to get out of the way. There was a coldness in the killer's eyes that had no give in it, and no chance of mercy.

Maya found herself thinking about her sister in that moment. She was doing this to save Megan, but now there would be no one left to do it. If Maya died, there would be no one to solve the Moonlight Killer's cases for him, and then he would have no reason to keep Megan alive, or any of his other bunnies.

Maya lay there, staring down the barrel that was going to end her life.

She heard a shot.

Maya waited for the pain, and it was a second before she realized that the shot had come from behind her. The killer jerked back, falling to the floor with the gun tumbling from his hand.

Maya looked around and saw Marco standing there in the open doorway, still sighting down the barrel of his weapon.

"How?" Maya said.

"I tracked your phone. I knew you'd go after the killer, and I couldn't let you do it alone," Marco said.

Another time, Maya might have tried to argue with that, but not then. Not when Marco had just saved her life.

They'd done it. They'd found the killer. It was over.

CHAPTER TWENTY NINE

At the precinct Maya started to clear away the office space she and Marco had borrowed. There was a kind of satisfaction in it, knowing that she was only doing it because she'd solved the case and put another murderer away.

"How long do you think it will be this time before you get a postcard telling you where to look?" Marco asked. He was across the room from Maya, collecting together files. He looked almost nervous about being there, as if he expected Maya to throw him out at any moment.

She wasn't going to do that, though, not after he'd just saved her life.

"I don't know," Maya said. "Probably not until I get back to D.C."

Which meant that until that point, a woman was sitting there, not knowing if she would be killed or not. It meant that Maya had to stay on edge, ready to speed out to the handover site.

"I should feel happier about this," Maya said. "I just caught a killer. *We* just caught a killer."

She added that last part because without Marco, this would have turned out very differently.

"Then why don't you?" Marco asked.

Maya found herself shrugging. "Maybe because of who Samuel was trying to kill. We've saved the woman who abused him. And for what, if she's dying anyway? She'll never face justice for what she did, her husband is walking free, because we can't show what he knew and when. It feels… hollow."

Marco shook his head, though. "If this were just about Delia Graham, maybe, but she wasn't the one whose murder you were sent to solve. Christine Weller and the others didn't deserve what happened to them, being murdered just for who they happened to look like."

Maya had to admit that Marco had a point there. If she focused more on the other victims, it was possible to feel some of the deep sense of satisfaction that normally came at the conclusion of a case. It was possible to remind herself that she was doing something valuable and important even if she was chasing around at the whim of a serial killer.

Maya knew that not all of the discomfort she felt came from that, though. There was still one other thing she needed to do.

"Marco, I'm sorry," she said. "I overreacted when I found out that you'd taken a leave of absence to be here. I know you're not trying to act like my babysitter, and that you're just trying to help with all of this."

"No, I'm sorry," Marco replied. "I should have told you about it from the start. And I should have trusted you to be able to look after yourself."

"Well, I think the part where you literally saved my life makes up for that one." If she still closed her eyes, Maya could still see the barrel of her own gun being pointed at her.

Marco came over and put a hand on her shoulder. "I wasn't going to let anything happen to you."

For a moment, just a moment, Maya felt the spark of a connection between them. It would have been so easy in that instant to just fold herself into his arms. Maybe even to lean in and let her lips touch his. The image of that was definitely clear in her head. She could almost taste him.

Yet Maya knew that she couldn't, not here in the middle of a precinct, and not when they still hadn't managed to get through a date without it going wrong. Maya found herself just standing there, looking into his eyes.

"Are you going back to Cleveland?" Maya asked.

She saw Marco nod.

"I don't want to. I want to be here with you. I'm in this for the long haul, but it's going to take time to swing it with my boss. But I'll definitely be there the next time that you need me, even if I have to quit."

Maya couldn't express how grateful she was for that. For now, though, she was going to have to let Marco go, and she needed to get back to D.C. She still had a woman to find.

*

Maya returned home to find a postcard waiting on her door, stuck in place with tape at eye level, somehow even more brazen than all the others had been. The sight of it there was enough to stop her in her tracks, staring at that small rectangle of cardboard.

It had a single bunny on it, with a bloody paw, shivering in the snow. Maya snatched the postcard from the wall, flipping it over to reveal the message from the Moonlight Killer.

Congratulations, Maya. You're proving to be all I had hoped. As promised, our bunny with the injured paw will be released. But hurry. She may be a little cold. Don't worry about the one who died. I'll find a replacement, so the game can play out in full.

There was an address below, in D.C. A feeling of dread filled Maya. When the Moonlight Killer said "cold" what did he mean? Had he killed her? Was *this* the punishment for the raid? To be sent out after a bunny, only to have her snatched away?

No, Maya had to believe that wasn't it. Otherwise, why was she doing this at all? Saving these women was the whole point of any of this, with the prospect of getting Megan back at the end of all of it the beacon that kept Maya moving forward.

Maya got out her phone and texted Harris.

I have a location for another victim. I'm heading straight there.

She texted the address to her boss, then turned around without even stepping into her apartment. Some things were far more important than an empty home.

Maya ran downstairs, then headed out to her car. She leapt into the driver's seat, and set off in the direction of the address from the postcard. Her GPS fed her directions, barely keeping up as Maya gunned the engine, speeding towards the spot where the bunny was waiting.

Maya took a left, skidded around a car, and found herself looking at an empty lot. No, not quite empty. There was a cargo container sitting in the middle of it, clean and new, in contrast to the graffiti adorning some of the walls there.

As soon as Maya's eyes fell on it, she knew where the woman she was looking for had to be.

She pulled into the empty lot, and even as she threw herself out of her car, she saw FBI vehicles coming up behind her. An ambulance came with them, and they fanned out around the shipping container.

Maya made sure that she was the first to it, checking for any sign of tripwires or pressure plates. Even now, she didn't put it past the Moonlight Killer to put a trap on the container.

There was a large padlock on it. Behind Maya, Harris, Reyes, and a couple of others were approaching quickly, but Maya didn't want to wait for them. If there was a woman trapped in there, then Maya wanted to get her out of danger as quickly as possible.

Drawing her gun, she shot the lock.

It broke, letting Maya tear it clear. She opened the doors, and a blast of cold hit her. She realized in that moment that it was a refrigerated container, with ice crystals forming around the edges.

There was a woman lying inside, shivering. She wore a dull gray boiler suit, and was curled in on herself, as if that might keep her warm. She was clutching her hand, and Maya could see the bandages there.

This was the woman whose finger the Moonlight Killer had sent. This was the one who Harris and the rest had gotten hurt. Who *Maya* had gotten hurt.

Maya ran over to her.

"Can you hear me?" she said.

She didn't get an answer. The other woman seemed to be too cold, or too traumatized, or both, to say anything.

"Hold on, I'll get you out of here."

Maya lifted her, half carrying, half dragging, her out of the container. Agents were approaching quickly, spreading out around Maya.

Paramedics came close, taking the by now semi-conscious woman from Maya's arms.

"We've got her, Agent," one of the paramedics said. For a moment or two, Maya didn't want to let her go, not so soon after finding her. Even so, she let the newly released woman go, passing her to the paramedics as Harris and Reyes moved to stand over her.

"Did you see who did this?" Reyes asked, leaning over her.

"Can you tell us anything about where you were kept?" Harris asked.

Maya couldn't believe the callousness of that. All they wanted was to find more information that might lead to the Moonlight Killer.

The paramedics were already moving off with her, and Maya was grateful for that at least. She didn't need this woman to be caught up in the FBI's attempts to catch the Moonlight Killer, whatever the cost.

Harris and Reyes barely seemed to notice.

"We'll wait until she's recovered," Reyes said. "She'll be hypothermic now, but a day or two in the hospital and-"

"And what?" Maya snapped, unable to help herself. "And what then, Reyes?"

"Easy, Grey," Harris said. "We're all on the same side here. We're trying to find the guy who did this. We'll get the information from this witness, and we'll go from there."

On another day, Maya might have let it go. She might have told herself that Harris was her boss, and that she couldn't afford to upset him. She might have told herself that there was too much danger of being pulled off this case.

Now, though, Maya found that she couldn't hold back that easily.

"No," Maya said.

"No?" Harris sounded as if he didn't understand.

"No," Maya repeated. "No more raids based on things I'm pretty sure the kidnapper is setting up. No more running into things and getting people hurt."

"With respect, Grey," Reyes said. "We all know why you're saying this."

"Because my sister is being held hostage, yes," Maya replied, squaring up in front of Reyes. "A fact that you love to throw back at me, but you never actually seem to remember when it counts. What has it been? Three times now that we've gone running after the kidnapper, and all it has done is get people hurt? The woman we just rescued is missing a finger, because neither of you would take no for an answer. Because we had to go looking for the kidnapper *again*, with no certainty that he was there."

Harris didn't look happy with that. He gave Maya a grave look.

"Remember that I'm your boss, Grey. If you don't like working on this, I can always transfer you to another department."

"And then the remaining women die, including my sister," Maya replied. She wasn't going to back down now. This had to be settled. "I'm the only one the kidnapper wants to talk to. If you stop me from working this case, you don't get anywhere."

Harris stared at her, looking as if he wanted to argue. The only problem was that there was nothing to argue with. Without Maya, there was no case.

"So we all just have to do this your way?" Reyes asked.

"Shut up, Reyes," Harris said, and that was sharper than Maya expected.

Reyes looked surprised, taking a step back.

"Sir?"

"Grey is right. The only contact we have with this guy is through her. I'm not prepared to put that at risk. And I'm not risking the lives of the remaining hostages."

"Thank you, sir," Maya said.

Harris gave her a hard look. "Don't thank me yet, Grey. It means that all of this is on you. You have to come through. You want us to do this your way, that means you have to succeed."

Maya could feel the pressure of that, but it was far better than the alternative.

"If that's the case, then I want help," Maya said.

"What kind of help?"

Maya took a breath. "I want Detective Spinelli of the Cleveland PD transferred to work with me."

"Sir-" Reyes began, in a tone of protest.

Harris cut him off. "Very well. And Grey?"

"Yes, sir?"

"There's one other thing you should know. A young woman, an artist, was kidnapped yesterday. One thing was left at the scene."

Harris held out his phone. On it was a picture. An artist's canvas sat next to a wall. On it was a painting of a single bunny, with the word "Maya" written underneath in bold letters.

EPILOGUE

Tori had never been more scared than when she woke in the cage. She stared at the metal of its bars in horror, her brain refusing to comprehend what was happening.

She stared down at herself, and saw the gray boilersuit in place of her own clothes. That brought a fresh wave of horror with it. If someone had done that, what else had they done?

"Help!" Tori cried out.

"Shh!" a woman's voice hissed back.

As Tori looked around more, she realized that there were other women in cages that seemed almost identical to hers: large enough to lie down in, plain and undecorated. She could see women in cages off to either side of her, and more across from her. Tori thought that she counted seven more in total.

"What is this?" she asked them, trying to keep the panic out of her voice and failing. "What's going on?"

One of them had fading bruises all over her face, like she'd been systematically beaten up by someone. She had dark hair and delicate features.

"Do you remember being kidnapped?" she asked, in a low voice.

Tori was about to say no, of course not, but then the van came back to her. The feeling of the man who had grabbed her, who had injected her with something, who had trapped her like a spider drawing a fly into his web.

She sagged back against the wall of her cage as a fresh wave of panic hit her.

"It's all right," the woman across from her said.

Another woman, a couple of cages down, made a sound of disbelief.

"It's not all right. We've been kidnapped by a madman. One who's going to murder us!"

Tori stared at her wide eyed. This woman was perhaps twenty-five, with long hair that had been dyed blonde, but was now growing back darker, showing how long she must have been in there.

"Haley," the first one said. "You're not going to be murdered. He just released Asha."

"That's what he says," Haley snapped back. "He says that this is all some grand game, that if some FBI agent solves cases for him, he'll let us go. Do you really think he's doing that? You really think he isn't just taking us out and killing us?"

She sounded frantic, scared and helpless in equal parts.

"It's real," the other woman said.

"Now you're saying that? When you've barely bothered to talk the rest of the time? He beat you. He made Asha cut off her own *finger*. He killed Carmel and left her body for us to stare at. He's playing with us, trying to make us suffer before he kills us. And I'm not going to play his game anymore."

Tori saw a flash of something then, there in Haley's hand. She realized that it was a piece of glass.

"No, wait," Tori said.

It was too late. Haley brought the glass down, slashing it through her own arm in a long vertical line from elbow to wrist. The kind of cut people made when they were serious about ending it. The kind that couldn't just be stopped with pressure and bandages until help arrived.

Haley gave a cry of pain, and sat down against the wall of her cage even as blood poured from the wound.

"Why?" the woman with the bruises demanded. "Why?"

"He's never going to set us free. At least… this way, it's *my* choice. Mine. Not his."

Tori heard the sound of booted footsteps running closer. A man appeared, masked and dressed in shapeless dark clothes, so that it was impossible to tell anything about him.

He worked with keys, trying to get the cage open. In the seconds that took, Tori saw Haley slumping down, blood pooling around her now, flowing out far too fast. Their captor managed to get the door open, going to Haley as if he actually cared whether she lived or died.

He crouched there, trying to hold pressure on the wound with gloved hands, but the blood wouldn't stop. It just kept flowing, and Tori saw Haley's eyes flutter closed, her breath coming shallow and fast.

Then she gave a shuddering gasp and went still.

Tori heard a cry, and realized that it was her voice. None of this made sense. She couldn't be there.

Their captor stood then, and his masked gaze swung over the rest of them. It fell on Tori for a moment, and she fell silent instantly. She couldn't see anything except the man's eyes, but those were enough.

She'd never seen the kind of cold anger that rested in those eyes before. Those were eyes that looked at her as if she were nothing. As if it were harder *not* to kill her than to do anything else.

In that moment, Tori understood exactly the kind of man who held them captive, and she knew that Haley had been right. There was no way that a man like this was ever going to let them go.

Not alive.

NOW AVAILABLE!

GIRL FIVE: BOUND
(A Maya Gray FBI Suspense Thriller —Book 5)

12 cold cases. 12 kidnapped women. One diabolical serial killer. In this riveting suspense thriller, a brilliant FBI agent faces a deadly challenge: decipher the mystery before each one is murdered.

In the Maya Gray series (which begins with Book #1—GIRL ONE: MURDER) FBI Special Agent Maya Gray, 39, has seen it all. She's one of BAU's rising stars and the go-to agent for hard-to-crack serial cases. When she receives a handwritten postcard promising to release 12 kidnapped women if she will solve 12 cold cases, she assumes it's a hoax.

Until the note mentions that, among the captives, is her missing sister.

Maya, shaken, is forced to take it seriously. The cases she's up against are some of the most difficult the FBI has ever seen. But the terms of his game are simple: If Maya solves a case, he will release one of the girls.

And if she fails, he will end a life.

In GIRL FIVE: BOUND, a serial killer takes one thing from each of his victims. Why? What do they have in common?

And whom will he strike next?

A complex psychological crime thriller full of twists and turns and packed with heart-pounding suspense, the MAYA GRAY mystery series will make you fall in love with a brilliant new female protagonist and keep you turning pages late into the night. It is a perfect addition for fans of Robert Dugoni, Rachel Caine, Melinda Leigh or Mary Burton.

Book #6—GIRL SIX: FORSAKEN—is also available.

Molly Black

Debut author Molly Black is author of the MAYA GRAY FBI suspense thriller series, comprising six books (and counting); and the RYLIE WOLF FBI suspense thriller series, comprising three books (and counting).

An avid reader and lifelong fan of the mystery and thriller genres, Molly loves to hear from you, so please feel free to visit www.mollyblackauthor.com to learn more and stay in touch.

BOOKS BY MOLLY BLACK

MAYA GRAY MYSTERY SERIES
GIRL ONE: MURDER (Book #1)
GIRL TWO: TAKEN (Book #2)
GIRL THREE: TRAPPED (Book #3)
GIRL FOUR: LURED (Book #4)
GIRL FIVE: BOUND (Book #5)
GIRL SIX: FORSAKEN (Book #6)

RYLIE WOLF FBI SUSPENSE THRILLER
FOUND YOU (Book #1)
CAUGHT YOU (Book #2)
SEE YOU (Book #3)

www.ingramcontent.com/pod-product-compliance
Lightning Source LLC
Chambersburg PA
CBHW030615310726
48979CB00003B/722

* 9 7 8 1 0 9 4 3 9 3 6 1 2 *